children of stardust

VOLUME 1

By: Iago Hyde

Book Cover by Iku-Aldena

Interior Illustrations by Pandabaka

ISBN: 978-1-7368891-0-7 (paperback)

ISBN: 978-1-7368891-1-4 (ebook)

overture

ABLANKET OF WEBBING WOVE itself over the god's estate, suffocating the screams that emanated from the mountain-top castle. Lifeless bodies were frozen as they had died, some running, some cowering. The countless spiders who had already cloaked the outside with their dark work now determinedly invaded the inside.

The insects' funerary cloth extended to every bit of the mansion; the winding hallways with their centuries-old artwork, the rooms that held revered artifacts, and the elegantly designed bedrooms all found themselves swallowed by the white spider silk. They took their time consuming the once grand estate, seeming to enjoy the splendor. Their movements were uniform, as though they were an army being led by some unseen general. The fine threads, their weaponry, glimmered across the corpses like freshly fallen snow.

Through the mansion's labyrinth of hallways, a servant boy in his early teens ran for his life. He wore only his sleeping clothes, and the webbing grasped at his bare feet with each step. Staggering into the estate's training room, he saw that his only option was to grab a wooden sword; others likely took the more threatening weapons before his arrival.

He wasn't sure what he could do with a simple wooden practice weapon, but his eyes held the determination of any warrior as he weaved through the halls, even as his hand on the hilt trembled. He dodged the bodies of soldiers and his fellow servants, refusing to look at any of them. The boy heard skittering on the walls and floor around him and, out of the corners of his eyes, he could see small shapes with elongated legs dancing masterfully over the web. His foot stepped on one and he felt the guts squish against his bare feet. Bile rose in his throat, but he stumbled on.

He turned down one hallway and saw an older woman screaming as she swatted at the uncountable swarm of spiders that crawled up her body. She turned to him and sobbed. Whatever she might have said was lost, for the insects invaded her mouth as soon as she opened it. She took a few staggering steps towards him, and instinctively, he stepped back.

While her body froze, the boy whispered a silent prayer. He had never thought he would watch his aunt die. Not like this. The web crawled up to claim her paralyzed body, and the spiders cascaded down—and began the quick race towards him. He pushed aside the memories of her that had briefly taken hold of him. There was no time to mourn. Instead, he spun around and kept running.

As he ran down another hallway, a door in front of him burst open. The head samurai, his face half-shaved with shaving cream still on his chin, staggered out. The boy couldn't help but stop; he had never seen this proud captain with such a look of absolute fear on his face. The man didn't notice him. Instead, his hands reached out for something — anything — to save him from whatever was inside the room.

"A Child of Stardust! Hurry, sound the alarms! Help-!"

His words were cut off as the boy watched the white webbing slither out of the room and wrap around his throat, dragging him back inside. His fingers grasped futilely at the edges of the door, but the door suddenly slammed shut—and the boy watched the man's severed fingers fall to the white floor.

The boy could feel tears running down his cheeks; he wasn't sure when he had started crying. He just knew that he had to keep going. Above all else, he had a duty to protect the deity of the estate. No one else could distract from that priority. There was no question of who was more important to save.

So the boy kept running, ignoring the sound of silken threads snaking about as they claimed more victims. Though his lungs ached, he kept moving. He only stopped when he had reached the side door of the meeting hall. This part of the estate had become silent. His breaths were deep and ragged, but they were not loud enough to overshadow the quiet sound of talking coming from the inside of the room.

He froze immediately. It had been burned into his skull to never interrupt the god when he was with someone. Even now, the fear of punishment for that disobedience kept him from bursting inside. His fingers shook as he brought them to the edge of the door frame. He did not open the door, but pressed his ear against it.

"It's been some time, Lord Yamamoto. You've lived a long life, even by a god's standard. I would have thought that your children would have succeeded you by now. Though when we met, you were practically a child yourself."

It was a feminine voice, gentle and polite. It was unfamiliar and it made the hairs on the boy's arms stand on end. He couldn't help the feeling that the spiders that had not yet reached this part of the mansion were now crawling towards his ears.

"My father may have been the one to fight you, but I've had hundreds of years to grow my power. I don't know what game you're playing, *Masamune*, but do not think your breed's tricks will work on anyone now!" Lord Yamamoto boomed, his voice like a sudden explosion amidst quiet chimes, and his words echoing through the space as strong and unrelenting as the stones he governed.

"Breed? Well, I am glad to know that you remember us so fondly. Is that why you were seeking the Wayfinder's Compass? If you missed me that badly, all you had to do was wake me-"

"You know why I want the compass. Weapons masquerading as people will not intimidate me-"

A whipping sound came from within the room. Then there was only silence. In the eerie peace, the boy felt his body go numb. Lord Yamamoto's words had been cut off. The boy wouldn't let himself consider what that might mean. He tugged the door open, daring to peek inside.

The main doors to the meeting hall opened at the same time. A pale woman in a teal and purple dress, her black hair tumbling over her shoulders and her mint green eyes staring dutifully ahead, entered. Her large black animal ears twitched at the silence, while a thick and fluffy tail stayed tight against her backside. Here, too, the spider web had covered the room and hidden the splendor that once existed there. Only the lanterns flickered with dying flames.

At the very back of the room, on a raised platform, stood Lord Yamamoto's corpse. It was still posed for an attack, his sword outstretched in frozen hands. In front of him stood another woman who appeared completely unbothered by his attempt at an attack; her casual stance made it seem like she was still in silent conversation with the frozen deity.

She was a tall, slender, and dark-skinned woman who wore a beautiful kimono that shimmered in different shades of purple. Her fine violet hair had been drawn up into an intricate sort of bun set in place by a pin with a black and pink spider-like symbol. Pink bangs framed her face, matching the color of the pin.

The black-haired woman bowed. "We found his information regarding the compass, my lady. Its location was the site of one of the Wanderer's last battles, just as we had guessed. I've gathered Aster, Nuwa, and Clementine. We will head out once you give the word."

She received a single nod in response and started to leave the room, but paused to tilt her head backward. She seemed to glance back at something, but the boy could not tell what. It was brief, and soon the green-eyed woman disappeared and closed the door behind her.

Back in the meeting hall, the elegant woman stepped towards the covered form of Lord Yamamoto. Her face held a subdued smile, but there was something in her glassy silver eyes that was terrifying to behold.

"Thank you for finding the Wayfinder's Compass for me. But know this, while the Children of Stardust might be weapons, I..."

She paused, and her head turned to look his way–to look, he realized, right at the door he was peeking out from behind. Had she truly seen him, despite his silence? She did not approach, but raised a single hand up, revealing the webbing extending from her fingertips in thin strands which connected to the threads all around her. He felt cold as her gaze never wavered from his spot.

The boy took a few deep breaths. He knew that it had to be now. Whoever this woman was, she had taken down the God of Stone. Who was he to challenge such a force? But who was he if he did not? She had claimed Lord Yamamoto's life. Even if he was destroyed.... Even if he became little more than a fly upon her web, he knew he had to fight. His hand went to the wooden sword at his side. His thumb brushed against the rough wooden shaft as he pulled the weapon out for the decisive battle.

"What do you think you're going to do with that?" A voice mused from behind him.

The boy turned and barely caught sight of the green-eyed lady. His lips parted, but no sound came out. His hand twitched and, in that moment, his sword was hacked into shards by wires that had wound around every part of his form. The sound of the wooden pieces hitting the white floor echoed within his spinning head. Laughter from the main room chilled him and his tear-filled eyes trailed over to look through the door, still ajar.

In the main room, the silver-eyed woman's smile grew wider. She stepped forward one more time and chuckled. Eight glowing purple spider's eyes blinked to life around her body.

"I will be a wielder."

She wrenched her fingers into a fist toward her chest and crushed the God's body with a sickening crunch. The blood from the body trickled down the pristine snow of webbing toward the woman. The sounds of thousands of spiders approaching covered the last strangled gasp the boy could give before his world became silken white.

chapter one

"We are all made of Stardust. Within all of us are the makings of a supernova, a black hole, a wish captured in a shooting star. We are all a bit of someone's dream. And we all have the potential for luminosity."

-Anonymous

"**F**UCK."

Roanoke Mochizuki woke from his nightmare and found himself holding a heart-topped pink staff that was ticking like a bomb ready to explode.

He fumbled with it until he located a small explosion sigil. It was the need to not blow up that gave him the power to push back the dark memories from his sleep. His thumb pressed down on the symbol until he felt it go from hot to cold, then he released it with a deep exhale.

Waiting until the pounding of his heart slowed, he then wiped the sweat from his brow. Roanoke had woken up from his dreams holding a weapon before, but.... The sound of FUKO's latest song reached his ears. It must have automatically updated to his playlist while he slept. He ran his hands over the staff as he examined the weapon and, for a moment, he tried to imagine a fighting style he could use with such a gaudy thing.

"Fuck detected. Good morning! Would you like to hear the top news for this sphere today?"

Wincing at the pleasantly robotic sound of his tablet, he tossed the staff to one side. It landed on a pile of other weapons he had yet to take care of, all results of his sleep-creating. At some point, Roanoke knew he would have to put them in the ship's mini storage plane, but for now.... He glanced over at his tablet and saw the holographic screen already displaying a list of news that he wouldn't be able to process until much later in the day.

"What's the ship's condition?" Roanoke asked, a yawn straining his words.

"Parked On: Sinner's Point. Ship Condition: Laughable. Crew Condition: Desperate. Monetary Condition—"

Roanoke quickly waved a hand over the screen. "Where are we...?" he whispered to himself.

He brought up a map of the area. Myth had insisted on continuing straight through the sleeping hours designated for travel through the Namid Sphere of the Stardust Sea. Given the wyvernboy's driving skills, it was questionable how far they had actually gotten. His rainbow eyes, shifting in various colors, scanned the image and found their dot. He had to zoom in and, when the place they were on finally appeared, Roanoke swore under his breath. It looked like a shady outpost amid a wealth of possible safe havens. He had, unfortunately, grown used to such side stops. Roanoke quickly changed and slipped a silver fetter inlaid with a glowing rainbow gem onto his hand.

Turning off his music, Roanoke stepped outside his room and nearly smacked into his pet. The little will-o-wysp, a bundle of Stardust formed into a ball, had been waiting outside his door to greet him. As soon as Roanoke realized he had slammed his chest into the little ball, he gasped and lurched forward to rescue them. The orb was hardly hurt by such a thing, however. They bounced off the walls and jumped energetically into Roanoke's waiting hands. As soon as they were safely there, Roanoke exhaled slowly.

"Geeze, Lil' Guy. For an emotional support familiar, you're causing me a lot of stress," he lightly chided the creature.

The will-o-wysp merely floated up to lounge on his shoulder triumphantly. The young man relaxed a little and slumped against one wall.

"Where's Kal and Myth?" he asked after a moment. The ship was too quiet.

In response, the will-o-wysp shot down the hallway and towards the closed door leading outside.

Suppressing a sigh, Roanoke continued down the thin hallway. He passed Kaleida's room, marked with several stickers and an open/close sign she had "borrowed" from an abandoned store on Camus. Myth's room came after that, the door plastered with a custom wanted poster the older man had gotten done of himself.

The storage room on the back wall was filled with the collectibles Kaleida and Myth had squirreled away. Its door was decorated with a basic touch screen that showed a condensed version of their entire inventory in neat little boxes. Roanoke held up his Chroniker and waited as it synced to the room. When the shrill beep confirmed the connection, he lowered his watch and began to browse through their stuff for some basic items for the day.

Of course, there was some unnecessary stuff, like the life-sized ice drake statue Myth had won in a drunk-fueled card game. Roanoke stared dully at the icon for it. His fingers lingered spitefully over the sprite.

What are we supposed to do with that?

Suppressing a sound that was halfway between a yawn and a sigh, Roanoke chose his daily amount of health potions. Noticing Kaleida had taken all the Diet HP, he reluctantly withdrew five Health Ups. They were more expensive than the Diet HPs, especially since Myth had gotten the Diet HP store-brand instead of a healer god-approved case. It was what they had grown used to. Figuring that his companions might have missed something, Roanoke also withdrew four Stardust energy shots and some Insta-Lights.

As he finished getting ready, the ship violently shook, accompanied by the screeching of metal. Even after it had stopped moving, Roanoke kept still as he crushed his emerging frustration. He took a moment to tie his white hair up into a ponytail, the dark blue and purple lower locks sparkling with starlight as they fell over his shoulders. As soon as his hair was set, he bolted into the communal space of the ship. The pilot's area didn't put him any more at ease. It was an open space in front of the communal area where, from his position, Roanoke could read the "FAST TRAVEL ERROR" sign flashing in a desperate plea for help on the pilot's screen. Lil' Guy bounced around one hand, silently demanding a pet before he would leave, and Roanoke obliged. After the pet was satisfied, the already-exhausted man opened the door and stepped out to see what chaos would be greeting him that day.

He had been right about the sketchy part. The air tasted of smoke from various unidentifiable substances. Sinner's Point was a barren and rocky place, not even big enough to be considered an actual star. It was an asteroid, no doubt acquired by some rich mogul during a buyout of the whole belt. Pathetic mountains poked out from the land, and, a short distance away from them, a deep abyss had been carved into the earth.

A lonely bus stop was proof that people did stop there out of choice, though the broken sign and flickering bus schedule screen it boasted did little to inspire any confidence. There was a small road that began and ended without ceremony, and on either side of it, shoddy abandoned buildings stuck out like tombstones. It was a dull, dark, and gray place. The only lighting afforded to it was the flashing neon sign signaling the rest stop just a short walk away from them. *Sinner's Point and Quick Mart*, it read, punctuated by a badly drawn logo featuring an arrow hovering over an asteroid with a smiley face glaring aggressively on the tall beacon.

Sadly, their ship fit right in. As Roanoke stepped out, he surveyed the exterior. It hardly looked like a ship at all, by more tech-progressive standards. In fact, it looked more like one of those motor vehicles with a living space that people would use to go camping. It was dented several times over by various attacks from the debris of the Stardust Sea, chipping away at the gaudy paint. The name of their clunker, Hazard, was painted on with glittering pale blue spray paint. It was thoroughly unimpressive by all accounts, and yet it had been their home for the past six months.

"We should've traded up!"

"I AIN'T abandoning her!"

Myth's Crazetusk drawl called out from the front of the ship. It took him only a few steps before Roanoke found the pair in the midst of one of their debates.

"I'm tellin' ya, I can fix her right up," Myth insisted, leaning over an opened hood that exposed the tech board interior. Smoke rose up from it and caressed the man's tired features.

He was dressed like some old-time space rancher, or perhaps a gambler, both of which he fancied himself to be. His clothing was a bright and obnoxious mess of colors, painted with graffiti. Out of all of them, Myth was the one who took the longest to get ready in the morning. It was a bit ironic, considering the man was constantly covered in the spray paint he worked with. Even his dreadlocks, in various shades of brown, were decorated with these splotches of color, and his hat was no exception either.

"And I'm telling you, we should just call Bong Cha." The other speaker stood on the other side of the hood, half-leaning over the edge of it. Kaleida Mochizuki, Roanoke's twin sister and Myth's partner-in-crime, held an already-triumphant smirk on her lips.

Like Roanoke, her features were sharp and she shared his pale skin and rainbow freckles. However, most of their similarities ended there. Kaleida's hair was fine and straight, cut to her neck. Her shorter bangs were black at the top before descending into a magenta galaxy pattern. The broad-rimmed hat on her head put Myth's to shame. It was a dark thing, but the neon accents on it were intricate and shimmering. Her outfit had a similar rancher feel, like Myth's, although Roanoke didn't know why she chose the look.

"Kaleida." Myth's tone was the one he used when he was trying, and failing, to act like her older brother.

"Myth." Kaleida's voice was cocky and playful.

"We ain't-"

"Hear me out. We call her up. She comes and fixes it up all nice, maybe even gives it an upgrade. We buy her lunch, and I casually remark about the view here and how she should stay a bit. We have a sweet moment together at the peak."

"Now we're spiraling!" The look on Myth's face already spelled defeat.

"I ask her out, she says yes, and--"

"Kal, please--"

"--Boom! Girlfriend unlocked."

Kaleida slammed the hood down victoriously, narrowly avoiding closing Myth in with the engine. Taking a moment to regroup, a mischievous look flickered in Myth's golden-brown eyes before he leaned back onto the closed hood.

"How 'bout this. We call up Bong Cha-"

"Yup, all for it."

"YOU tell her the ship went out again."

Kaleida paled. "Wait, no-"

"Hear me out. YOU explain to her why she had to come all the way out here to fix up somethin' she's already worked on ten times now. And YOU get to tell her how we don't have the money to pay her for her time and effort... again."

Defeated on the rebound, Kaleida turned away from Myth. She caught sight of her unfortunate brother, who had stood by awkwardly throughout the fight, and walked up to inspect him more closely. She immediately frowned with concern and realization.

"Mornin', Roan. Did you have that dream again?" Kaleida asked quickly.

"You ain't confessin' anythin' to anyone with that kind of attitude. Mornin', Roan." Myth grumbled and turned back to face his ship.

Roanoke wasn't in the mood for Kaleida's well-intentioned attention. Instead, he walked past her and up beside Myth. He examined the tech board and the sparks coming off of it as though he understood any of what was going on there. Roanoke had a little info about a lot of things, but almost none of it was related to advanced technology. It didn't help that the ship had recently been upgraded with low-level Technomancy, courtesy of the subject of Kaleida's hopeless crush.

"What's wrong with it this time?" Roanoke kept his gaze downward, but out of the corner of his eye he saw Myth slump a bit.

"Overheated a bit. Her engine core ain't likin' the new tech Bong Cha shoved in there."

"Without that tech, we wouldn't have an inventory space at all." Kaleida flashed Myth an accusatory look, to which the man threw his arms up in the air.

"I ain't sayin' she did wrong or anythin'. Just sayin' it ain't mixin' nice."

"At this rate, this ship's not going to last six more months. It's a miracle we've been able to drag it around the Sphere so far. We have to call Bong Cha." Roanoke decided, the result of his pointless examination culminating in what he already knew. Behind him, he could hear his sister jump in the air and could just imagine her fist raising in triumph. "You're going to call her." Roanoke added, and felt the smallest sense of satisfaction as he heard her deflating.

chapter two

THE GROUP TOOK A STRATEGIC retreat after the dreaded call to Bong Cha from the broken-down ship into the convenience store with an attached diner. The store carried a number of less-than-appealing items. Expired healing potions, cheap Stardust energy shots, and various clearance Stardust-enhanced items that were more like toys than anything of use. Though the trio had lingered slightly in front of the snacks and drinks section, the growling of their stomachs called for something more substantial and they had soon slipped into the diner.

It was just as empty and decrepit as the convenience store. As they entered, Roanoke noted the way it felt frozen in time. Scattered around the space were newspapers that had been tossed aside and that no one had ever bothered to pick up.

LIVING WEAPONS: THE TRAGEDY OF THE COS
SIGHTED: COS ANKAA DESTROYS THE TITAN OF
RIGEL
ASHEN SEEK EQUAL RIGHTS IN SEIEUNGHA
TECHNOMANCY: NEW MAGIC BLENDS
TECHNOLOGY AND STARDUST

The titles stuck out, and the young man couldn't help but scan them critically. The Children of Stardust.... He was getting sick of hearing about them. He couldn't linger on the news, however. Kaleida grabbed his arm and yanked him along.

As the three claimed an uncomfortable-looking booth in one corner, he silently took in a group of thugs that had taken over a space in the back of the diner. They weren't anything too special, more like caricatures of the kind of punks found in every corner of the solar system. They were noisy and comfortable and obviously had nothing better to do than hang out in a place that no one else would bother with.

But as the trio sat, the group glanced over at them and Roanoke could sense an undercurrent of unease. Kaleida and Myth, far more natural in a space with people, didn't seem to notice or care about the group. Of course, Kaleida was slightly more distracted as she brooded over the call that she had made just a few minutes prior.

By the time Roanoke turned his head back from his surveillance, Myth had already kicked his boots up on the table and Kaleida had grabbed one of the paper menus. She held it up in front of her face like a shield, preventing the world from seeing the way her eyes welled up with large tears.

Roanoke watched her for a moment, feeling reassurance rise up in his chest that he couldn't put into actual words. Instead, hopelessly, he smacked Myth's feet off the table and nodded his head at her.

Myth and Kaleida had been best friends for the past two years. Surely he would know how to-

"I've seen her madder. Remember last year, when you destroyed her-"

Oh no.

"I mean, ya blew it up and she practically-"

Roanoke's gaze drilled into Myth in a desperate warning.

Stop.

Kaleida's body practically shook with anger as Myth spoke. Unable to take any more, she slammed the paper menu down on the table. Given how light it was, the action was far less dramatic than she probably would have liked. Still, her prismatic eyes shone with fire and her tears had disappeared.

"This comforting thing you're doing? Not working."

"Me comfortin' means payin' for lunch. How 'bout you, bud?" Myth smiled at Roanoke as he threw him under the bus.

Asshole.

Roanoke was saved from having to come up with a passable answer, however. He opened his mouth and-

"Turn it up!! I'm tryin' to hear this shit," one of the punks, a boulder of a man—and one who was actually made of a boulder—shouted.

He smacked one of his friends who cradled a basic radio broadcaster, and obligingly the volume was turned up to an obnoxious level.

"One month from today will mark the two year anniversary of the release of the Children of Stardust, often referred to as the CoS. We are still left with many questions about their revival. Who freed them? Why? In the absence of answers, they have quickly become the universe's most wanted criminals. Gods of every domain from almost every star have scrambled to take proper safety precautions. Their reappearance has also prompted many adventurers to seek out the Teien artifact known as the Wayfinder's Compass, which has long been rumored to be able to track the weapons. Tonight, Consul Hemlock of LI Alliances will be on to discuss her organization's stance and plans for dealing with these criminals, as well as how they have been cooperating with the P-300 in this matter."

Under the table, Roanoke tugged the edges of his sleeves over his silver fetter, hiding the shimmering Prismatic Core gem that adorned it. He stared straight ahead at his companions, his expression neutral and giving nothing away. An awkward silence filled the space, and Myth looked between the twins before putting his feet back on the table.

"Next month... ain't that your birthday? The big eighty-four. You Teien age mighty strangely. It's still weird to think that you guys were practically senior citizens when I was just starting to grow hair on my chin-"

"That's still a work in progress," Kaleida said, a slight grin returning to her face.

"I'm just sayin'. It's a whole guessin' game every time we meet one of ya. It can be hard to guess someone's age if they look like they're thirty but they're actually like a million years old."

"And how many of us have you met?" Kaleida gave him a knowing smile.

"Enough to be confused. If ya'll weren't so scattered across the stars—"

"Excuse us for being nearly extinct." Kaleida stuck out her tongue and, in a good-natured fashion, she elbowed Myth in the gut.

As usual, Kaleida didn't bother to give consideration towards her naturally unnatural strength, causing Myth to double over as the hit rattled his ribs. A moan of pain escaped the man's lips, and the group in the corner glanced their way.

"Be quiet," Roanoke scolded them and smacked Myth's feet off the table once more.

"Tell that to the radio." Myth chuckled weakly and settled for resting his head against the cool plastic of the table. "They keep puttin' out those broadcasts and we're gonna have more competition than leads."

"Having leads isn't the problem. We know it's somewhere in this system." Roanoke's gaze showed just a bit of weariness. "The transportation is the-"

"Problem? Nah, Bong Cha will have her fixed up right as rain, soon as she gets here." Myth gave Roanoke a pitiful wink, rewarded only by an eye roll from the "younger" man.

"And in the meantime?" Roanoke's eyes had wandered to gaze out the window they sat in front of. As his rainbow eyes drifted towards the jagged gap marking the nearby abyss, he thought he could hear a faint melody echoing from it...

"In the meantime, we explore!" Kaleida said decisively. She scrambled over Myth's body, crushing the already beaten man into the back of the booth as she wiggled her body out. Narrowly avoiding falling flat on her face, she stuck the landing and spun around on the tips of her toes to flash them both an excited look. "There must be something interesting here..."

With a practiced sigh, Roanoke took his usual post as the joy-killer. He brought out his tablet and pressed a button, watching as the stats for their current location sprung up. It was sparse at best, depressing at most.

"Sinner's Rest Stop. Gods: None. Tech level: Minimal. Stardust level: Minimal. Interest level-"

"Minimal. I get it. But you know what? There's a thousand ships going to every star in this system looking for the same compass we are. And this place? Empty." Kaleida made a broad sweeping motion of her hands, using the diner as her proof.

From their corner, the thugs scowled at the group that dared to be almost half as noisy as they were being. Roanoke instinctively tensed. The feeling of eyes on him always made his skin crawl, and his fingers dug into the cloth of his pants.

"We don't have time, Kal. Six more months without anything to show, and we're officially terminated. This place? It's nothing," he said, careful to keep his tone quiet and even.

"It's an opportunity. Come on, Roan, we don't have anything else to do!"

Myth began to put his feet back up on the table, but a quick warning look from Roanoke caused him to pause.

"Kal's got a point, ya know." Myth shrugged.

"Roan, you read way more than I do. You know that if there's a bunch of signs pointing you one way, then the other way's the right one." Kaleida's eyes had become big and puppy-like, the hallmark of a sibling trying to get another sibling into trouble.

"And if we can't leave until Bong Cha gets here, then it's that or take up space in this diner," Myth offered.

The trio fell quiet once more. They took in their surroundings with a new sense of absolute boredom. One could practically see a tumbleweed rolling by. Roanoke sighed deeply. If he were fighting one or the other, then he could hold his own. But when Kaleida and Myth teamed up, like they typically would, then there was little he could do in the way of combating them.

His mind lingered on their goal. Getting the Wayfinder's Compass was the priority. It had been the priority for six months, aside from the slim hope that they would be lucky enough to run into one of the Children of Stardust while traveling. Myth's Stardust-infused luck abilities, however, did not extend that far. Overall, it seemed more and more like the group's total luck had been depleting for some time. There really was nothing else to do until Bong Cha arrived, and if it kept the pair busy and out of trouble, then...

"This isn't an adventure." Roanoke weighed each of the words he spoke. "But I-"

Kaleida gave a shout and grabbed Roanoke's arm. She wrenched the poor man out of the booth and onto his feet. Her arm looped around his in what felt more like a handcuff, and she beckoned with her free hand for Myth to follow.

"Myth, toss the money down! We've gotta go!"

Myth paused, half-way through getting out of the booth, and pursed his lips. The man glanced about the diner until he spotted a server golem left broken and abandoned in one corner. A tacky "Out of Order" sign had been looped around its neck.

"We ain't even ordered..." Myth grumbled.

"Myth, Come on!!" Kaleida's voice called out from the doorway insistently.

Resigned, Myth tapped a button on his watch. He quickly looked over his bank balance and put a hand over his chest. Roanoke felt for him, knowing that Kaleida's warped sense of manners wouldn't be satisfied until they left money for taking up space in a restaurant. With trembling fingers, Myth punched in the amount to be withdrawn. The interstellar marks appeared in his open hand in a neat little bag, which he placed on the table with the same air as one leaving flowers on a grave. His solemn task done; Myth hurried to catch up to his teammates as Roanoke turned and looked ahead.

AS they left, the leader of the thugs called his pals to attention. The others had been scoping out the money left behind, but his dull gaze had followed Myth with mild interest until they caught sight of Kaleida... Or more specifically, Kaleida's back. On the jacket's backside, a very controversial symbol had been beautifully woven into the cloth. The group of troublemakers began discussing what they would do if they could.

Unnoticed by all, one table set against the windowed front wall of the diner held another occupant. Slouched to the point of laying down across the ripped up booth, a young man with wispy pale grey hair and a layered grey and red outfit seemed quite content with his nap. His face was hidden by another old newspaper. ***THE WANDERER: HARBINGER, CRIMINAL, CREATOR OF CHAOS*** was a dynamite headline and apparently an adequate sleeping mask as well. A sturdy black guitar case was propped up against his table and gentle music came from a pair of headphones on the man's ears. All in all, he was a thoroughly unimpressive figure that matched the subdued and passive setting.

The unchecked noise of the thugs stirred the sleeping beauty. One gloved hand slowly moved to take the newspaper off of his face. With soft features and pale skin decorated with small bars of black metal, the young man could have been mistaken for a ghost of the diner. Ghosts, however, did not have to try and sleep through the half-witted plans of men. The faint music that came from the man's headphones could not block out the sound of trouble. The young man seemed to decide to confront the problem by avoiding it entirely. The bundle of grey and red cloth slipped silently out of the diner and out of the way of any sort of adventure.

chapter three

THE REST OF THE TOWN WAS AS thoroughly uninspired as the diner and convenience store had been. Most of the small structures that remained in the area were empty and abandoned. The "street" was nothing more than a space between the two rows of buildings. As Roanoke stood in the center of it, and the town itself, he looked around with a flat expression and pondered just how Myth had seen the place to begin with.

"Roan, I found a gift shop, c'mon." Kaleida's firm hand grasped at his arm and she tugged him along once more. They soon entered one of the empty buildings. It was, as she had said, a gift shop. However, nothing in it felt like gifts. Layers of dust covered the shelves and counters spread throughout the place. Most of the items had long since been taken out of the small box of a store.

"How does this look?" From one corner, Myth held up a bright pink t-shirt with *I SURVIVED SINNER'S POINT* printed in obnoxious orange lettering. He held it over his chest and flashed the pair an eager grin. "Since this place is all shut down, I bet no one'd mind if I took myself a souvenir."

"You're not bringing that back to the ship." Roanoke walked past him to survey a row of evil-looking ooze plushes.

"I don't know, I think he'd look pretty sexy in it." Kaleida gave a dry snort and made her way over to examine some cracked snow globes.

"Ya'll are cruel." With a dramatic sigh, Myth placed the shirt back and continued to walk around. "Ya think they'd have the compass in here? Maybe it's on sale." He flashed the twins a dry grin, causing them to roll their eyes in unison.

"Sure. Thousands of people are searching for a compass that just so happens to be stuck in some box at a rest stop." Roanoke furrowed his brow as he came to a stack of postcards. He shifted through them idly.

They were about as pathetic as postcards could come; there was nothing that could be considered scenic or eye-catching about the asteroid. Most of the postcards were of the nearby stars instead and the few that were of the asteroid were poorly shot, as though they had hired some random person to take the photos instead of a professional.

As Roanoke pulled out one card, however, he paused. The picture itself was relatively simple. It was one of the few postcards that were drawn, and it had been done surprisingly well. It featured the peak at the edge of the abyss which he had been looking at earlier. Standing at that point, their back to the viewer, was a hooded figure in a white cloak. The cloak seemed to ripple in a non-existent wind, and the back of it featured a familiar symbol. The golden circle with curved lines connected to a smaller circle in the shape's interior, and within that, a brilliant peacock feather's eye. It was the infamous mark of the Wanderer, the same symbol that adorned his sister's back and hair. The bottom of the postcard read, ***Come stand where the Traitor once stood!***

"It seems I've caught you with your guard down, Roanoke Mochizuki. I knew this day would come."

Roanoke stiffened as he felt pressure against his back, but it lasted only a moment before he recognized his sister's voice. His rainbow eyes glanced up at a dirty mirror atop the postcard stand and, through it, he could make out his sister grinning mischievously at him as she held a foam sword pointed at his back. His eyes glanced back down and he noticed a basket containing more. The smallest of smiles spread over his features. He slipped the postcard into his pocket and brought his hands up in submission.

"And what do you think you're going to do now that you've got me?" he muttered with a defiant tone.

"Perhaps I'll ransom you. Perhaps I'll just keep you hostage until your knight in shining armor—"

Before Kaleida could finish her words, Roanoke had lunged forward. He grabbed two of the foam swords and held them at the ready as he pointed them at her. His sister blinked with surprise before she readied herself.

"Clever. But you haven't escaped yet." Kaleida gave a loud and wicked laugh that seemed to come from deep within her gut.

Myth winced at the sound; he had approached the pair when the noise had started, but quickly realized he didn't want to get involved. The man did a quick turn and went back to observe the pink shirts thoughtfully.

"Give it up. You know I'm better with swords than you," Roanoke retorted. They danced around each other as they kept their distance with the dull blades raised.

"Prove it."

Kaleida's voice was the drop of the flag, the firing of the gun, the signal to start. In an instant, Roanoke had lunged forward. His skill with the swords was nothing less than fluid. Kaleida held her own as she defended against every blow he delivered, but he pushed her back with wide swings of the two swords. The battle quickly extended to the rest of the store as they continued their fight through the aisles.

"You've gotten slow!" She rolled out of the reach of one of his swings and into an aisle.

"You've gotten cocky." Roanoke turned the corner to find her up and running away. With a deep breath, he took after her once more.

Her aim was obvious: she was on the retreat. Apparently willing to abandon her passive crewmate to Roanoke's possession, she shoved Myth at Roanoke as she passed him and ran to the front of the store. As she reached out towards the handle of the door, it swung open in front of her and nearly caught her in the face. The thugs from the diner stood in front of the doorway and glared down at her with indignant fury.

"You! You know what you're wearing?" The boulder man stepped forward, murky grey eyes glaring daggers at Kaleida.

The young woman merely smiled in response, though her eyes were hard. "Well, hello to you too."

Roanoke frowned instantly. It didn't take a genius to read the space and sense the danger that had just pushed their way in through the door frame.

"I asked you a question, bitch."

Kaleida laughed despite herself, glaring up at the man with a smile on her lips. "A jacket? Or maybe you're asking about my exceptional hat? Sorry to tell you, but it's custom made and-"

"You got that fucking symbol on your back!" The thug leader snapped, and a bit of sand dripped from the corner of his mouth. Slowly, Myth and Roanoke approached the entrance.

"Is that illegal?" Kaleida taunted.

"Maybe not, but it oughta be! You're asking for trouble."

The symbol. The damn symbol.

Roanoke seethed internally. He had told her not to wear it many times, but she was stubborn and insisted that she needed to show her support for the Wanderer. He was never sure if it actually accomplished any kind of support, but it did get them in an unnecessary amount of trouble.

"Ain't no harm bein' done here," Myth ventured. His hand went down to a deck of cards in a holster at his side. Like Kaleida, he smiled at the man with hard eyes.

"It's the Wanderer's symbol! That monster's done enough harm in this universe! That symbol's a fucking curse. Do you even know what it means?"

Kaleida stepped forward until her chest practically bumped into his lower stomach. The fire in her eyes and the tense posture of her body promised a fight, though her grin never wavered.

"Do you?" she asked, tone defiant and proud.

"It means anyone who wears it is supporting a star-killing, CoS-making maniac!" The boulder man's enormous fist swung at Kaleida's head.

Kaleida ducked to one side. The man's movements, while powerful, were slow and awkward. It was the fighting style of one whose primary experience came from drunken escapades. Despite the wide miss, he used the opportunity to force his way completely into the gift shop. His followers, a group of five punks wielding various makeshift weapons, followed him and stood off against the three. As one of them slammed a bar against a nearby newsstand, Roanoke winced and stepped forward.

Before Roanoke could make his move, Myth pushed past him and stood in front of the twins.

"Ya'll need to chill." He drew his deck of cards out of its holster and flashed the others a challenging grin. "I ain't afraid to show ya how."

As the twins watched, Myth's eyes glowed with a power that extended to his deck. The top five cards in the deck shot up into the air and spun around in front of the gambler. He made a face at the selection, and Roanoke could tell immediately that none of the cards were his top choice. The thugs stopped in curiosity at the display, though as Myth made no further movement, the boulder man growled.

"The fuck you doin'!?" He brought out his own iron club and pointed it at Myth.

"Well, ya know, I just... was admirin' my hand..." Myth grabbed one card and held it out with a forced chuckle. "Three of diamonds." The rest of his cards slipped back into the deck at his proclamation

Kaleida leaned towards Myth. "Isn't that the card that—"

In front of Myth, three giant spikes shot out of the ground at the thugs as the card disappeared. The spikes, made of a powerful created metal, tore through everything in the gift shop. Everyone in the small space scattered at the display of power until the spikes shot their way through one wall and to the outside.

In the remains of the shop, Roanoke groaned and forced himself out from under some shelves that had fallen. He saw Kaleida and Myth doing the same a short distance away and glowered at the latter.

"That was the best option?" he hissed at Myth, spitting out a bit of the ceiling as he did so. When Myth gave him a resigned shrug in response, Roanoke turned his attention to the thugs who were regrouping.

"What, we throw a punch at you and you use Stardust against us!?" The leader looked offended, and Roanoke found he couldn't really blame him.

It had been a large reaction to a relatively minor act, but he also knew it was probably the least violent card that Myth had gotten from his draw. Roanoke rose to his feet. It seemed like his skill would be the best for the present problem. However, as he held out his fetter-adorned hand, he realized he was still holding the foam swords. He made a face, and the hesitation was just enough time for one thug to act.

Out of the corner of his eye, Roanoke saw movement. The iron edge of a thin club connected with his stomach and sent him rolling towards the hole that Myth had inadvertently created. As pain momentarily left him winded, he heard Kaleida shout.

"Hey! He hasn't even done anything yet! That's it."

Roanoke tilted his head to look at his sister. Kaleida had jumped onto one of the collapsed shelves and stood proudly over them. "You want to see Stardust? Fine!"

She took only a quick glance around the area before she found what she needed. Like Myth, Kaleida's rainbow eyes glowed powerfully. The thugs had advanced on her, but a new sound stopped them. Fluttering filled the partially destroyed space. Old newspapers and sales ads that had been scattered by Myth's attack flew up in the air and spun around them.

"Kal, wait..." Roanoke groaned.

Kaleida flicked her wrist and the papers turned into paper airplanes. They rushed at the thugs within the store, stabbing at them with surprising roughness. However, her control over the airstrike was less than complete. As she launched her attack, several of the paper missiles shot in random directions. They stabbed into the walls and the few remaining standing structures in the store. As some flew particularly close to Myth, the gambler yelped and ducked behind a piece of wall.

The thugs struggled as they tried to combat the attacks. It was obvious they had been in no way prepared for this as they fell over themselves to get away. They scrambled outside of the gift shop through the hole, most of them barely avoiding Roanoke. He had almost gotten to his feet when the boulder man hoisted him in the air.

Roanoke looked down at the ground, which was suddenly a blur underneath him. It took his dazed mind a few moments to process the fact that someone had grabbed him, and that a rocky arm was wrapped tightly around his waist. His arms were clamped at his side, still holding the two foam swords.

"Roan!" Kaleida screamed.

But the boulder man had him facing the opposite direction of the store. His features burned red with embarrassment over being so easily grabbed, and also utter disgust at being touched at all. He struggled against the larger man, but even his own slightly inhuman Teien strength fell short of fighting an actual rock. The sensation of having someone else holding him made bile rise in his throat and he continued to writhe.

He had been so focused on his attempted escape that he didn't realize how far the gang had moved until he stared at a row of single rider motor-ships. The smell of fuel stung his nostrils and, as the thug kept him close to them, the loud engine roars nearly deafened him. His heart pounded faster in his chest, but indignation was replacing his panic.

The leader of the thug attempted to pull Roanoke inside with him, but the young man kicked his feet at the opened door to hold him back. "Where the fuck do you think you're going to take me!?"

The other thugs had stopped, and they hovered around their own ships as they watched.

"He's got a point, Craid. You plannin' on kidnapping over this? What the Tartarus are we going to do with him?" the one who had first hit Roanoke asked.

"Oh, you'll see."

The boulder slammed Roanoke's head into the side of the door and his world spun once more. Dazed, his resistance fell just enough for the man to shove him in. As he was left haphazardly in the backseat, he heard the thug leader get into the ship as well.

"I'm gonna drop him! You keep those two busy." the man shouted out the window to his friends.

The ship roared once more as the boulder started the engine and drove off in the abyss's direction. Cries of protest and reluctant agreement mixed in the background. The sounds were soon cut off, however, as Roanoke could hear paper whizzing through the air and stones being displaced.

"Where is he!?" He heard his sister call out as his companions engaged in battle once more.

Roanoke grunted as he tried to sit up, but the world continued to spin every time he moved. The sound alerted the thug leader, who glanced back at him just long enough to give a smirk. "You think you can worship the Wanderer and not get your shit wrecked? Enjoy the fall you're gonna experience real soon."

"I'm not..." Roanoke tried to protest, but the man turned away from him.

He narrowed his eyes as the boulder turned on the radio and blasted a heavy metal song to drown out his sounds of pain. As soon as the music hit him, his spiteful gaze grew wide. He could feel his fetter growing warmer with power. The Prismatic Core inlaid on the top of it glowed a mix of green and yellow and the two foam swords in his hands started shake.

Fuck.

AT the pitiful bus stop by the abyss edge, the grey-haired guitar wielder had comfortably settled down on a sadly standing bench. The very act of sitting on it caused the bench to creak and groan in pain, but the young man tested his luck further by laying down completely on it. This was, apparently, the straw that broke the camel's back. As soon as he had found the most comfortable position the bench had to offer, the mess of wood and metal gave out entirely. He gave no sound as he suddenly found himself lying in the remains of one of the few markers of the bus stop's existence. For several long moments, the man simply laid on the stone earth and contemplated the development.

Finally finding the motivation, he rose to his feet and nudged at a few of the pieces with his foot. He clasped his hands together and evidently gave a silent prayer for the loss of the furniture. It was a somewhat comical gesture, but it was done with such a passive and solemn air that it appeared he was being genuine.

The prayer finished quickly enough, and the musician gathered up his guitar. He placed it on his back and stepped away from the bench, only to hear the sounds of fighting and the speeding of a ship. With reluctant movements, he turned to see a full-on brawl occurring just outside the diner where the motor-ships were parked. The thugs he had heard earlier were clashing with two of the travelers. As his pale red eyes scanned the scene, however, he became keenly aware that there were two particular people missing... and that there was a ship heading directly towards him.

The ship was completely out of control, and for good reason. Through the front glass of the ship, the musician could see flashes of lightning. It spiraled out of control, and he saw it slam into the tall sign in front of the convenience store. As it did, the thin metal broke and the silly grinning meteorite arrow on top fell.

The more pressing matter, however, was the ship: it slammed into the ground just a short distance in front of him. He was spared any damage from the crash, but he was the only one. The pilot, covered in cuts and burns, shrieked and scrambled within it until the glass finally shattered and the boulder man rolled out. Jumping out from the ship after him was the white-haired young man he had seen earlier in the diner. He stood, wounded but firm, with two electrically charged serrated-edged swords in his hands.

"You dumb mother—" the white-haired man stopped as he noticed the musician.

At the moment's hesitation, the seven-foot mountain of a man rose and swung his fist at the sword wielder. He leaped back until he was beside the grey-haired man. Beyond them, they could see the two young adventurers rushing to join at their side, leaving behind a mess of beaten-up ships and thugs. The boulder, noticing it, pulled out a somewhat basic but still deadly pistol. It was larger than a regular pistol, appropriately sized for the bigger man, with bullets that would no doubt leave a giant hole in an average person.

"You destroyed my ride," the thug hissed.

"That's worth being shot at?" The young man growled back, but his injured body was shivering with the effort to remain standing.

Out of the corner of his eye, the grey-haired man noticed the status bars on their Chronikers. Both were low. The world seemed to slow as the man cocked his gun and aimed it at the Teien. His two companions were just a little too far away.

The musician sighed.

Fuck.

THE sound of the gun firing reverberated in Roanoke's gut. He had instinctively blinked at the sound, but when he opened his eyes, there was no wound or bullet. Instead, a grey-haired man stood in front of him. It had happened faster than Roanoke could see. Had the man moved while he blinked? It was the only way that he could have missed the quick exchange. Roanoke hardly had the time to process it. The grey-haired man staggered past him without a sound, obviously in some kind of daze.

"The edge—!" Roanoke cried out.

A faint song played in his head as he watched the man tumble forward. It dug at the edges of his mind, but he continued to stare at the musician unflinchingly. As his body disappeared over the peak, Roanoke felt his blood run cold.

Without thinking, Roanoke jumped forward. He peered into the darkness that was welcoming the falling figure. The two swords, remnants of the former foam weapons, fell onto the stone floor. He reached out towards the man. There was no thought in his mind, no hesitation. The pounding in his heart was his only guide as he grabbed the musician's hand.

Roanoke's prismatic eyes connected with the musician's pale red gaze. He thought that he could see a silent, questioning look in those endless eyes. He felt his feet leaving the rock as the force of the other man's fall took him along. He made no sound but, behind him, he could hear Kaleida scream.

He was aware of the feeling of his free hand being gripped by someone — Kaleida? — but it only halted his and the other man's fall for a brief, sweet moment. Soon they were plummeting once more.

"Kal! Roan!"

Without hesitation, Myth grabbed onto Kaleida. Like a chain of idiots, the four cascaded over the edge of the cliff and down into the deep abyss below.

AS the bodies were swallowed by the darkness and Kaleida and Myth's screams faded, the thugs who had claimed their ships screeched to a sharp stop and looked at each other. The worried and confused gazes finally turned towards their leader. The boulder man was silent for a moment as he, too, stared over the edge and into the darkness.

"Let's get out of here! I ain't sticking around to explain to the LI Alliance how their bodies got down there!" he finally snapped, shoving the gun back into his side pocket.

Those words were more than enough to convince the others. The boulder man was left with no choice but to ride in the back of another's ship. The group of thugs sped away, and Sinner's Point fell silent once more.

chapter four

AT THE VERY BOTTOM OF THE abyss, where the feeble light from above could not reach, were two figures entirely unaware that a group of would-be adventurers were falling to their death above them. One sat upon a gathering of rocks that had fallen from the walls of the abyss at one point or another. They were a rather interesting figure, short and lithe, covered in layered ornamental clothing that had natural tones and colorful accents. Bird feathers and beads adorned their body, and a simple headband made an attempt to keep a mess of spiky red and orange hair in place. Mischievous green eyes that stood out vibrantly against darkly tanned skin were currently directed down at the newspaper that they were holding. The headline read: ***COS MAYURA DESTROYS TRISTE KING'S MONARCHY.***

Despite the rather ominous headline, there was a bright grin on the figure's features as they read the article. A light-hearted giggle escaped their lips and they eagerly looked up at their companion. They waved the newspaper in the air rapidly.

"You're getting more and more famous! You keep going after those big bad people and pretty soon you'll be a real villain!" the small figure chirped like a bird.

They were ignored by the second figure, a young man who was pacing back and forth on the floor of the abyss. His bare feet made soft sounds against the earth, and he stopped only to pick a sharp piece of rock from his skin every now and again.

This preoccupied man was a somewhat striking counterpart to the first. He was tall and had the build of a dancer, which could most certainly be confirmed by the revealing dancer's garb that he wore. His chest and muscles were exposed, and most of his legs could be viewed as the pants had deep cuts in the sides. He was absolutely stunning, his willowy form nothing less than beautiful. Waves of blue, teal, green, and gold adorned his body, as did a wealth of jewelry and accessories. Long and wavy teal hair with faint golden sparkles had been brushed mostly over one shoulder with some braiding on the opposite side of the head to help guide it. A golden headpiece drew attention to the already eye-catching face. Vibrant purple eyes peered out, filled with annoyance, as he appraised both equally empty and barren paths before them. In one hand, a golden fan with peacock feathers for the interior lightly rapped against his arm.

The first figure allowed the second to pace back and forth three more times before accepting that the other was simply not going to give them the attention they wanted. With an exaggerated and loud groan, they fell backwards, letting their back hit the wall of the abyss. They had been down there for quite some time now, and had not gotten anywhere. The green-eyed newspaper-reader felt their paper-thin patience growing even thinner.

"Maymay, here's a suggestion: Flip a coin. There's, like, a million around here." Their voice echoed throughout the space. There was some merit to their suggestion, if only because they truly were surrounded by a wealth of different coins, faded and of various stars, that were scattered about.

While the words did not succeed in stopping the other figure, they did at least cause some reaction. The second figure glanced over at them and made a face.

"Leave them be. I'm sure if I concentrate hard enough, I'll be able to sense it."

At that moment, the first one heard screams echoing faintly through the abyss down to their location. The purple-eyed man seemed too far in his own head to notice it, but the first figure instinctively looked up. They could make out four distinct forms diving towards them like awkward birds who forgot how to land.

"Maymay-"

"I'm trying to concentrate."

The first figure looked back at their friend with an expression that seemed halfway between grumpiness and excitement.

"Maymay, I have another suggestion. You should look up!" they said, once more speaking loudly enough that it echoed through the abyss.

The second figure obliged with an eye-roll. As he did, however, his keen eyes also noted the falling bodies. He tore his gaze away to look at the first figure, then at their surroundings, and then back again.

"Hide, now!" he snapped, and jumped back towards the red-haired figure.

"But what if they need help? It doesn't look like they're flying," the newspaper holder grumbled, but the beginnings of concern were apparent in their bright green eyes.

The purple-eyed figure paused. Indecision was clear on his features, which furled into a deeper frown. There wasn't much time to decide. After a moment, the second figure gave a noise that only frustration could produce. He gave a wave of his fan, and a burst of magical Stardust-infused golden feathers swirled around them. The figures shimmered for a moment, then disappeared entirely. Despite their sudden non-existence, the second figure's voice clearly, and moodily, rang out.

"We'll see how they handle it. If they get within ten feet of the ground, I'll step in."

FIFTY feet above the ground, the group was far too preoccupied with figuring out how to survive than to worry about what might be on the cold hard rock waiting for them below. In the chaos of the fall, Roanoke instinctively pulled the grey-haired man to his chest, clinging to him like a lifeline. It most certainly wouldn't help stop the fall, but it fit the natural inclination of a falling person to latch onto anything at all. Kaleida still grasped her brother's jacket with one hand, but her free hand flapped as though she might suddenly develop the ability to fly Above her, Myth had let go of Kaleida's hand in order to save her hat, his other hand clutching his own. The group fell in the absolute darkness, barely able to see each other.

"Kal! Do somethin'!" Myth shouted, his southern Namid accent and high-pitched scream blurring his words.

"On it!"

Kaleida's eyes narrowed as she focused. With her free hand, she tapped the watch on her other wrist. She had to press it a few times, her flailing during the fall making it difficult to retain a sense of accuracy. As she finally hit the right button, her personal inventory screen appeared. Her finger slammed down on the first item in the inventory: a stack of 999 pieces of paper. The bundle appeared with a glow in her hand, and Kaleida immediately tossed it.

The papers fell around the group and her prismatic eyes glowed with power as she concentrated. The rainbow shine extended to each piece of paper that fell around them. They moved with purpose, forming into a net that latched onto the jagged purple walls of the abyss. The group was caught by the netting, tumbling against each other in a tangle of bodies. There was an outpouring of protests as they tried to separate themselves, though Kaleida popped her head up through the mess with a bright grin.

"See? No problem," she said, shouting over the voices around her.

Roanoke managed to raise his head, his eyes narrowing slightly at her. "Kal, I don't know if this will hold-"

The distinct sound of ripping paper pierced the air. The twins stared at each other and, for a moment, slight triumph flickered in Roanoke's eyes. Kaleida, on the other hand, glared at him.

"If you hadn't said anything-"

The paper tore completely. The bottom of their literal safety net gave out and the group resumed their fall towards certain doom. The screams continued uninterrupted; all of them could see the hard ground coming closer and closer to their fragile bodies.

Suddenly, however, the air around them grew controlled and concentrated. It was no longer rushing past them. Instead, the group felt cradled by the wind. It caught them and they sagged into it as though it were the best air mattress in the universe. For a wonderful moment, the group was held in this way above the ground, then the air bubble popped and they fell unceremoniously to the ground.

Kaleida was the first one back up, leaping nimbly to her feet and looking around with wide-eyed excitement. As Myth started to rise, he held up her hat first, and she snatched it up to place it back on her head. He grunted as he stood up to join her. The area around them was dark, with only faint outlines as their eyes adjusted to the dark. The darkness did not last long. The glow from Kaleida's watch pierced it as she opened her inventory screen.

"Shit. I forgot to grab Insta-Lights. Roan, you got any?" She tapped the inventory screen away and switched to a status screen.

Roanoke chanced a glance towards her and the projected screen. Judging by the bright red line dictating her health, the thugs above hadn't been able to do a thing to her. However, the pretty glittering blue line that indicated her Stardust level had depleted, and she made a face.

Roanoke's attention shifted back on the young man in his arms. He sat up once they landed, still holding him. As he examined the grey-haired boy, he realized something fairly alarming. The young man's eyes were closed, and he was limp in Roanoke's arms. Panic began to swell within his gut. His mind echoed with memories kept at bay. He forced them back and quickly began examining the other for injuries.

"H-hey, you okay? C'mon—" Roanoke said quietly, but urgently.

He gave the the grey-haired man a shake. There were no signs of wounds or broken bones or anything, but he wasn't waking up...

Oh.

Roanoke's eyebrows twitched with annoyance. A quiet snore from the other man confirmed his thoughts. The grey-haired stranger had, in fact, decided to take a nap during their dramatic fall. Embarrassment flushed Roanoke's features, and he let the other man drop to the ground.

"What kind of fool falls asleep when they're falling to their death?" he hissed, and slowly rose to his feet.

However, he couldn't shake his confusion over the man's status. He had literally taken a bullet for him, and a large one at that. Yet there were no holes or signs of injury on him. It didn't make sense...

Kaleida hopped over as Roanoke spoke. Her watch allowed just enough light for her to catch a glimpse of her brother and his companion, and her rainbow eyes were wide with curiosity as she examined their slumbering hero.

"He's sleeping? That's so cool. I wish I could fall asleep that easily," she said, awe apparent in her voice.

"Ain't that the truth." Myth chuckled, brushing off some of his clothing as he made his way in their direction.

Roanoke put his head in his hand as his friends spoke. He sucked in air and slowly exhaled it before looking around. Finally recognizing that it was too dark, he opened his inventory screen and drew out one of the Insta-Lights that his sister had forgotten. It was a small orb, dark and ordinary at first glance. He tapped a small symbol on it, and it flickered on. The light was surprisingly strong, and it floated up into the air to hover over them.

"Aha, I knew you'd bring one, you over-preparing dork." Kaleida gave her brother a grateful look.

"Not over-preparing if you actually need to use it, idiot," Roanoke muttered.

He observed their surroundings. It was as he had thought. The bottom of the abyss held nothing within it. The walls were mostly jagged and certainly not easily scaled in either direction. The air around them was stale, and.... A thought popped into Roanoke's head.

"Anyone know what that sudden wind was?" he thought out loud.

His sister gave a shrug. With the light provided, she was already fluttering about to examine everything around her. "Maybe it's windier at the bottom of the abyss? Like a super ultra-air current?" she offered.

"That's so stupid I don't even know how I should argue it," Roanoke groaned.

"All I know is that if I were some fancy ancient compass, I wouldn't want to be stuck down here," Myth sighed. He cracked his back, eyes straining as he looked back up to where they had fallen from.

"And neither do I. We need to find a way back up. Kal, how many papers do you have left?"

"About two stacks. But that net cost me a bit of Stardust... Plus there was the newspaper scuffle." Kaleida pouted.

She opened her inventory screen, despite already knowing what was in it, and browsed through it to show her brother. The two stacks of paper were there, as well as her trusty shotgun, the foam sword, and some health potions. There were a few other odds and ends, but nothing that seemed to be absolutely helpful at the moment.

"If I tried to make some stairs, they wouldn't last long enough to get all the way back up. And I'd have to do an awful lot of concentrating to make them stay long enough to get everyone up. I could make Ori-Bird, but that would take a ton of energy and I don't even know if she'd last the trip."

"In other words, we're stuck down here." Myth took his hat off to run his hand through his thick hair, his expression dropping to a pout that almost mirrored Kaleida's. A heavy silence fell on the group as they considered the development. "What about you, Roan? You look pretty rough."

"Grabbing an HP soda and booster now." Roanoke dug the two out of his inventory and held them out so Myth could see. He tossed one to Kaleida, then downed both, enjoying the bit of extra time to think as he listened to his companions talk.

"We could-"

"I say we go exploring. I mean, we're already down here, right? And the whole reason we went exploring was because we-"

"You-"

"WE thought that the compass might be here. Look, none of us have the ability to get back up there like this, and no one's going to come looking for us down here. So our only chance of getting out is to get moving."

"I don't think—" Myth began to protest, but suddenly his golden-brown eyes lit up. He knelt down and picked up a coin, then two, then several more. "Aw, look at all these beauties! C'mon, I gotta replenish my stock..." He cooed to the inanimate objects.

"Oooh, is this a treasure horde?" Kaleida rushed over to join Myth.

Though she did not bend down to pick them up, she began pointing out various coins and identifying them by their star. If there was one thing he could say about his sister, it was that she certainly was more traveled than Roanoke. Still, the display of knowledge only brought a sigh to his lips.

"Seriously, is no one going to think about that wind?" he muttered, though he was already defeated. "They're just coins..."

"They're people's wishes."

Roanoke jumped at the unfamiliar voice. The trio looked back to see that the grey-haired man had woken up. He walked towards them, adjusting the guitar case on his back as he did so. Roanoke hadn't noticed it before, but surprisingly, the case had made it through the fall completely unharmed. He chalked it up to the wind that no one seemed to want to acknowledge. Still, as the man came up beside him, his anxiousness began to set in. He took a few steps away from the man and immediately looked elsewhere. Suddenly, the coins on the ground had become much more interesting.

"What do you mean? Is that some kind of legend?" Kaleida walked over to them, flashing her brother a look that silently told him to behave.

"If you want to call it that. The abyss at Sinner's Point has always been a popular spot to toss a coin in and make a wish." The young man's expression was neutral, but his eyes were soft as he looked them all over. His accent was familiar to Roanoke; it was likely a dialect from the Seieungha Sphere, though he couldn't be sure of the exact region. "Sinner's Point got its name from a battle a very long time ago. This is said to be one of the last places the Wanderer fought before his imprisonment. For some reason, people began to see that as a reason to toss coins into the darkness and make a wish."

Roanoke's eyes widened slightly. Without thinking, he brought one hand to the pocket that still held the postcard. The rumors that they and many others in the universe had been following had revolved around a similar story, but no one had known for sure which star exactly that battle had taken place on. To think that the Wanderer had been here.... His heart began to pound heavily in his chest.

"How do you know that? Who are you, anyway?"

The young man turned to face Roanoke, who was still avoiding eye contact. He said nothing, and Roanoke felt impatience mixing with the churning questions inside of him. With a faint huff, Roanoke finally faced the man directly.

"I asked how you knew that. In all the history logs and texts I read, it said the battle had taken place on a star, not an asteroid. What makes you so sure it was here?"

The man gave a small shrug, but his gaze stayed trained on Roanoke. It was a quietly powerful look, and Roanoke found that he was losing the will to continue maintaining his own gaze.

"I'm not sure of anything. All I'm saying is that history isn't concrete. There are many different histories and many different history books. The same story can be retold a hundred ways. That's all," the young man finally answered. His voice was so quiet that there was no echo in the space.

"Then we're on the right track! This is perfect," Kaleida gasped.

There was nothing worse than someone giving Kaleida affirmation for one of her stupid ideas. Roanoke opened his mouth to object, but thought better of it. His shoulders slumped as he realized that, no matter what he said, this had become a full-fledged adventure.

As her brother brooded, Kaleida held out one hand towards the grey-haired man. "Seems like you're stuck with us now, too. I saw you jump in the way of that bullet for my brother. Your guitar case blocked it, right? Pretty impressive to have a case that toughThat's a pretty expensive case, right? You a famous musician or something?"

"You're assuming a lot," the man said after a moment, giving the faintest of sighs.

Roanoke chewed the bottom of his lip as he turned his attention to the man's guitar case. *Was that what happened?* He hadn't even seen the guitar case move, and there was no sign of the bullet striking it. It wasn't like Kaleida to imagine that sort of thing, though.

"I'm fully registered to assume," Kaleida gave Myth another playfully rough elbow to the gut, which caused the man to double over. "Show 'em, guys!"

The rainbow-eyed paper-wielder tapped a few icons on her watch and a stat screen appeared with her basic information on it, as well as a badge that had a giant red X over it. The stats, which listed her strengths, abilities, age, health, and other factors, were faded and inactive. Myth reluctantly did the same to show his own, though unlike Kaleida, he seemed embarrassed. Roanoke didn't bother. He didn't want this man knowing his intimate details, and he didn't see the point in parading around the symbol of shame that his sister clung to.

"We're certified P-300 trainees!" Kaleida proclaimed proudly.

"It says expired."

Roanoke winced as the young man spoke, but he couldn't help but feel a little surprised. There was no judgment in the tone used, no laughter or cruelty. Instead, the voice held only a passive curiosity. Not quite questioning, but considering. It wasn't the usual reaction that they would get every time Kaleida flashed her badge, but-

"That's just a technical issue." Kaleida's face flushed in a way that very obviously said she was lying.

Roanoke couldn't help but give a dry snort at that. The reaction warranted a disapproving look from Kaleida and a quick shake of the head from Myth, but the young man gave him the faintest of smiles.

"We're looking for a compass," Kaleida continued.

"They sell compasses at the mart up there. I'm sure you'll be able to find one that actually works."

"Not just any compass. We're looking for the Wayfinder's Compass. It's-"

"The thing that will find a CoS." The young man shifted his guitar case on his shoulder absently.

"So you know what it is. Perfect! You're now obligated to help us find the compass while we're stuck here. Welcome to our mission." She gave him a winning wink.

"Is getting into fights with rest stop punks a part of that mission?" the young man murmured, raising a single eyebrow.

"Look, it's not our fault some assholes have a hang up about a symbol. It's not the first time someone's picked a fight with us over my jacket, and it probably won't be the last. But their prejudice isn't my responsibility." Kaleida shrugged and waved her outstretched hand more insistently in his direction.

The young man didn't take it, but instead looked around thoughtfully. For a moment, his gaze lingered on one area of the abyss, where a large piece of rock jutted upwards. The corners of his mouth twitched, but then he looked back at Kaleida and his shoulders slumped just as Roanoke's had.

"I ain't gonna complain about having the extra help, honestly," Myth called back to the others.

He had momentarily paused when it was first announced that the coins on the ground were the symbols of people's wishes, but his moral battle had been swift and he had apparently come to the conclusion that his empty wallet took priority over people's past wishes. As he shuffled along the ground to collect coins, Roanoke and the grey-haired young man observed him, the former wearing a slightly disappointed look on his features.

"That's interesting," the musician whispered. He walked forward and knelt down on the ground near some of the coins, letting his black-gloved fingers trace over the coins and earth below.

"What? Are you going to start collecting, too?" Roanoke felt a new sense of disapproval and unease rising in his gut at the prospect of another money-hungry person joining them.

"Roan, hush." Kaleida elbowed him in the gut.

Once more, her superhuman strength caused her motion to have more of an effect than she had intended. Roanoke, however, was a little bit sturdier than Myth and he merely flinched. He exhaled through gritted teeth, annoyance replacing his earlier disappointment. It was enough of an action to keep him silent for the time being. His eyes remained on their reluctant new companion, studying him like a pouting cat instead.

"There used to be a river here." The young man motioned for Roanoke to come forward. "Your light, please."

Reluctantly, Roanoke obliged. The Insta-Light dancing above his head followed him as he walked forward and knelt down beside the other. His rainbow eyes studied what the grey-haired man had pointed out. The coins were collected in a slight pattern that went both ways on the abyss floor. The stone, too, had been worn down. Smooth pebbles could be found among the coins. It truly did seem like water had flowed through the area at some point in the past.

"How did you see that?" Roanoke murmured in spite of himself. He had been looking at the same thing that man had. Why was it that some random person they found sleeping at the bus stop seemed so much more knowledgeable than him?

"A river. That's cool. I wonder where it went?" Kaleida mused, but her attention was elsewhere as she followed Myth.

"Usually this sort of thing happens when a river has been blocked up," Roanoke said quickly as he rose back up to his feet and looked around. "Who knows where that happened, though."

"Uh huh." Kaleida's attention was already elsewhere. She walked over to their new recruit, who was also just starting to rise to his feet. "You know, I don't think we've gotten your name yet."

They hadn't, in fact. Kaleida grinned victoriously as she enjoyed figuring something out before Roanoke had. It was a very rare occurrence and one that he knew she would cling to for later bragging.

"You haven't." The young man looked down at her with the same neutral, but slightly curious, expression.

"Well, I suppose we haven't introduced ourselves either. We should get on that. We did kind of drag you into this." Kaleida motioned to Roanoke and Myth, neither of whom seemed to be concerned about introducing themselves.

"Who's fault is that?" Roanoke grumbled, and Kaleida elbowed him once more.

"Fate's, so shut up. Anyways, my name's Kaleida Mochizuki. I'm a Teien and my special skills are paper manipulation and rifles. The guy over there doing the bend and squat for coins is Myth Lawson, and he can do a bunch of random stuff with playing cards. And over there's—"

"Roanoke Mochizuki."

"My grumpy twin brother. He can create weapons, and his glove—"

"You don't have to do this." Roanoke glared at his sister.

The fact that she was so willing to just give out their abilities drove him up a wall. Not only was it a terrible strategic choice, but he hated any stranger knowing more about him than absolutely necessary. His thoughts flashed back to the foam swords and the fetter. Back in that ship, the effect of his fetter had been helpful. But he didn't want to broadcast the skill. If someone knew what he could do, then they would also know all too well what he couldn't—

"It's part of the recruitment process." Kaleida smirked, then looked expectantly at the grey-haired man. "And you are...?"

There was a distinct moment of hesitation as the man looked over the trio. The corners of his mouth dipped ever so slightly into the faintest of frowns, but there was no other indication of emotion on his features. Even his eyes stared dully ahead.

"...My name is Sungmin Park." The young man turned away from the group and his gaze settled back on the small gathering of rocks.

"Sungmin Park, the musician of the team. It has a great ring to it, doesn't it?" Kaleida gave a firm nod. She gave Sungmin a pat on the shoulder, causing the soft young man to wince.

"I never said-"Before he could finish speaking, Kaleida was already on her way. Myth, willing to oblige his partner-in-crime, followed her obediently. The two passed by Roanoke as the young man stood still. As Kaleida walked by him, Roanoke was surprised to see a deeply thoughtful look on her features. Her rainbow eyes glanced back towards Sungmin as though she were unsure of something. For a moment, Roanoke wondered if she was doubting her own invitation. He wanted to ask further, but he didn't have a chance.

As the pair started off in the direction that Kaleida had randomly picked, Roanoke bit his lip. He would have preferred to study both paths more closely before they chose a direction, but more often than not, his desire for research was off-set by his sister's instincts. It wasn't as though there was much to examine, anyways. It was the bottom of a ravine and both paths looked nearly the same. That was how he viewed it, at least. But Sungmin... Roanoke glanced his way. What were those eyes seeing that he wasn't?

"Have you guys thought about calling for assistance? Your Chroniker is still working." Sungmin motioned to Roanoke's watch. "Someone with a fast enough ship could-"

Roanoke began walking forward before Sungmin could finish his sentence. He kept his eyes straight ahead, scolding himself inwardly for having stared at the man long enough to cause him to think he wanted a conversation. At the same time, he couldn't help but feel a pang of guilt. He wanted to say that it wasn't really Sungmin's fault, though the man did unnerve him. But being around someone new without his friends to provide some buffer was difficult. It always had been.

Being with other people outside of the close-knit group he had worked hard to form was nerve-wracking. His anxiety had gotten even worse since the incident, too. Without Lil' Guy at his side, it was all just a bit too much for Roanoke to take. He wanted to tell Sungmin that they had someone coming, but she was the only one who would be able to get there anytime soon, and she was still many hours away. He wanted to tell him that, even if there was someone, his sister was so bull-headed that they would have continued on either way. And he wanted, more than anything, to tell the man thank you for defending him when he had no reason to back up above. But the words wouldn't form on his lips. As he heard him start his music in his headphones once more, Roanoke felt even more nervous and picked up his pace. If that man was truly a musician.... He bit his lip. Though he kept walking forward, he did chance a look back.

Sungmin, for his part, didn't seem very offended by Roanoke's sudden departure. It was difficult to gauge his thoughts from his features, but he simply watched him leave. Then, with a shrug, the young man put his headphones back on over his ears and began to blast a new song as he followed after the group. The words of his song echoed faintly throughout the space, as though it was coming from the abyss walls themselves.

AS the group made their way down the path that had been randomly chosen, a curtain of golden feathers parted the illusion that had previously hidden the two figures. The taller one gave an indignant huff and stamped his bare foot against the ground. As he did so, his foot met a sharp rock and he swore quietly. Looking slightly less intimidating cradling one foot and balancing on the other, he nevertheless was righteously annoyed as he stared out after them. At his side, the smaller figure looked on with a laugh. It was a sweet and high-pitched noise that greatly contrasted the quiet swears and grumbles of the other. Finally, though, the first figure straightened out and tapped his fan against his side.

"Did that boy see me? I think he saw me. How did he see me?" the man grumbled, as though fully expecting that his friend would have the answer ready and waiting for him. "I am the king of illusions! It's an insult. No, it's worse than an insult. It's boring." He stamped his foot for extra effect, though this time he took the time to look where he was stamping.

His friend yawned and gave an eye-roll; it was obvious they were used to the taller figure's tantrums. "Uh-huh, okay. And what does the king want to do about them?"

The taller figure stared after the strange group. Their expression became less indignant and more thoughtful. In the silence, the shorter figure looked up at their companion. It wasn't often that their friend was so quiet for so long.

"They mentioned the compass. I'd say this was an issue, but they seem hopelessly ragtag. Still..."

"Still?" The shorter figure leaned up as they attempted to peer into the peacock's eyes.

"I say the coin has been flipped. We're going to follow them," the man said firmly.

Beside him, the green-eyed figure grinned widely. "This is gonna be so much fun."

chapter five

U NSURPRISINGLY, WALKING THROUGH a long, thin, and dark ravine was a relatively boring task. The group had traveled for an hour or so and, in that span of time, Roanoke had begun to read while walking. It was a somewhat impressive ability and one that he had cultivated when he was very young. The activity put him a little further behind Kaleida, whose long legs and broad steps practically dragged poor Sungmin along beside her.

Roanoke's company was Myth, who had continued to bend down periodically to pick up coins. The further they had progressed, the more Roanoke had begun to notice the curves and bends of the former river that they were walking along. The temperature of the asteroid was cool, and he had wondered what could have caused a river to fade away like that. Curiosity and a need to occupy his time with something had led to his reading. He brought out his tablet and was currently searching one of his preferred universal archives for any information regarding the place they had broken down on.

History isn't concrete... Sungmin's words rang in his head. He had read a lot of books, particularly regarding the history of the Wanderer. More than that, he had heard many stories about the infamous god from his family, so he ought to know better than anyone. It was not enough.

Beside him, Myth gave a dramatic gasp of air as he stood up from a squat. The man flashed Roanoke a proud grin as he shook his coin purse. He had certainly collected a heavy amount of people's wishes in the time they had been walking, and Roanoke would have questioned the man's dignity if he wasn't keenly aware of their current bank account. It didn't matter that these were star-specific coins, which would be hard to transfer into interstellar marks. It certainly didn't matter that people had tossed the coins into the abyss for a reason. And yet, Roanoke had to remind himself not to be too harsh on him. Both he and Kaleida had come from some measure of privilege, but Myth's background had been more difficult, from what his sister had told him.

"Phew. My thighs are gettin' a workout." Myth laughed good-naturedly, giving the side of his hip a light slap. He flashed Roanoke a goofy smile, and Roanoke rolled his eyes and tried his best not to return it.

"Too bad the rest of you isn't," he said coolly, but it was a harmless jab.

"Mean. I ain't the one who got us stuck down here."

The pair paused as they looked ahead at Kaleida, who was still chatting Sungmin up. The grey-haired man was quiet and patient as he listened to her, but the faint sound of music still coming from his headphones made it questionable if he were actually hearing anything that she was saying.

"She's your sister," Myth said after a moment, giving a shrug.

"She's your partner," Roanoke retorted with a huff.

Back at the P-300 Academy, it was standard practice to pair up trainees for various tests and missions. Kaleida and Myth had been the perfect pair since their first test in their first year. Roanoke, on the other hand.... He wasn't much of a team person.

"I don't want him in our group." Roanoke's rainbow eyes sparkled with pain that Myth noticed. That was one thing that Roanoke appreciated about the man. While he was sometimes oblivious, at the end of the day, he did understood the twins.

"It's just for this mess. Don't get ya head all in a tizzy about it, a'right? We're gonna get out of here and she'll get it out of her system."

Roanoke paused for a moment at Myth's words, taking a bit of time to process the word "tizzy".

Who uses that kind of word anymore? In spite of himself, a smile twitched on Roanoke's features briefly.

Ahead of them, Kaleida had gotten into another round of talking. As she walked, she gave sweeping waves of her free arm at the purple-ish rocky walls around them.

"I've been in worse spots than this."

"Oh yeah?" Sungmin encouraged her patiently.

"Oh yeah. Much worse. I was raised by the toughest P-300 Shikaaree this side of the Namid Sphere. Took my first steps in a dungeon off Rigel."

"And your baby bottle was a health potion."

Kaleida stopped and grinned at Sungmin, giving him a slap on the back. "How'd you guess?"

"Shot in the dark," Sungmin replied, his body lurching forward at the powerful hit. He showed no indication of pain on his features, though both Roanoke and Myth winced for his sake. She looped an arm around his once more and continued her cheerful parade forward.

"What about you? Any dashing escapades? What about a life-changing encounter?"

"Nothing to speak of. Sorry. I'm a boring person." Sungmin's attention had drifted as he studied the walls around them.

Kaleida came to a halt as he spoke. Without realizing she had stopped, he walked a few steps forward and was nearly yanked into a fall by her steadfast position.

"No one in this universe is a boring person, Sungmin," Kaleida said in a rare serious tone. Her rainbow eyes drilled into him and his face showed the faintest hints of surprise before he looked back at the walls once more.

Roanoke looked up from his reading to see what Sungmin was staring at. Along the rocky walls were veins. Despite being dull in color, with the Insta-Light orb hitting them, they could see the veins' galaxy-like appearance. It was as though the Stardust Sea had been captured in strains and solidified in the walls. It meant...

"Crystallized Stardust." Sungmin completed Roanoke's thoughts for him. Roanoke blinked, and noticed that the man was staring at him.

Kaleida and Myth finally turned their attention to where Roanoke and Sungmin had been looking. As they examined the beautiful veins, Kaleida walked up to one. Her hand reached out to touch the vein, but she seemed to think better of it and pulled it back.

"What're these doing here? They're so big... they could have been mined and used for so many focus symbols and items..." Her eyes seemed to shine as they reflected the vein.

Sungmin glanced behind them. He stared at the empty space that they had just passed through, then shook his head and looked back at the rest of them.

"Asteroids are generally mined for their crystallized Stardust. It's hard to find it on any star, and asteroids are usually unpopulated so there's no danger of harming native inhabitants. They are said to come from the creation of the Stardust Sea, themselves-" Sungmin explained, but Myth cut him off with a laugh.

"We know all that, kid. It's appreciated, but we don't need a basic lesson. I think Kal was just askin' why it's still here if there's a rest stop and all that up above."

"Who knows?" Unbothered by being cut off, Sungmin's red eyes once more drifted back behind them, as though that would hold answers.

Kaleida and Myth had a point, Roanoke realized. If the area above had been populated, and the asteroid belt bought out, then it would have made sense for the veins to be scouted out and mined. Veins that big could give someone a huge boost to their natural Stardust levels and allow them to use more spells, more items, more... well, more of anything that used Stardust. Roanoke looked from the vein to the rocky earth below them.

"What if the river was hiding them?"

The group looked his way, and a faint blush passed over Roanoke's features. He cleared his throat, turning his gaze back to the crystallized Stardust.

"If the river was originally higher, and it was long enough ago that they didn't have the same technology we do, then it would be hard to tell that the veins were here."

"The Stardust would have shined through the river, making it look like a reflection of the Stardust Sea," Sungmin added. "People at that time would have thought that's all it was. That might be why they tossed the coins in."

"And by the time the river disappeared, people didn't care enough to seek them out. I mean, if that rest stop up above was any indication, then this place-"

"-was abandoned by anyone who might have known or cared about what they were looking at." Sungmin and Roanoke stared at each other.

Poor Myth and Kaleida could only look back and forth as their teammates played verbal volleyball.

"It's still weird that the river's gone though, right? Like, the sun didn't dry it up, and this place doesn't have any oceans so... Uh, what else could get rid of a river?" Kaleida finally offered.

Sungmin gave a nod of agreement. "It's unusual."

"The river could have been blocked up." Roanoke took a few steps forward, running his hand along one vein as he did so. "It could have-"

A shock of energy surged through him as his fingers touched the crystallized Stardust. It was enough to make him shudder, as though he had touched a live wire.

"Roan?"

He heard Kaleida calling out to him, but his head began swirling as darkness peppered with flashes of light struck him. The vein was filled with power and memory, and both surged through him at once.

He looked around and saw that his team was no longer there. Instead, ghost-like people moved about the space.

"They finished blocking up the source yet?

"Obviously, dummy. We're not standing knee-deep in water anymore, are we?"

"Look, I'm not the idiot that thought it'd be a good idea to put something like this all the fucking way down here. I mean, who's going to want to come explore a place like this? No one. I'm getting paid to be here and I don't even want to walk around."

"Yeah, well, we'll be heading back up those stairs soon enough now that the job's done."

"Too bad they don't have us mining those veins. Maybe if the boss hadn't sunk his money into building this damn thing, we might've made some nice coin offa the Stardust."

"Speaking of coins, you see all these beauties on the ground? I don't think anyone would mind if we..."

The figures faded, and Roanoke blinked and found himself slumped against the wall of the ravine. The others had gathered around him.

"Roan? You awake now? What the Tartarus happened?" Kaleida knelt down at his side. She brought one hand up to his forehead and he frowned at her.

"I don't have a fever." He swatted her hand away.

"Let me be concerned about you, dumbass. You can't expose yourself to Stardust like I can. You don't have the control!" she growled, then paused as she heard her own words. "Hey, sorry, I didn't mean—"

"It's fine. I know." Roanoke sighed deeply.

He felt the edges of his ears burn red with shame and embarrassment. She was right. He shouldn't have touched it, but he also hadn't thought that the crystal veins would have that much power on the surface level.

"What did you see?" Sungmin asked Roanoke quietly.

Roanoke frowned at him, surprise flashing over his features.

How did he know...? Roanoke shook his head. *Forget it.* He was quickly discovering there was no point in asking how the man knew something. Apparently Sungmin just had an omniscient knowledge of everything.

"It was the past, I think. Some workers talking about sealing up the river, and how they couldn't mine the veins. They were talking about building something, though. And they mentioned something about going back up some stairs..."

Roanoke pushed himself up and wavered a little as the ripples of remaining Stardust coursed through him. Curious, he opened his watch and took a look at his status. As he thought, his Stardust bar had grown more powerful. It wouldn't be super useful to him, as long as things went alright, but it did tell him that the veins were still good.

"I didn't know a vein could make ya see stuff." Myth looked over at the crystallized Stardust thoughtfully.

"Stardust veins can sometimes absorb the echoes of past events. Things that have happened never truly leave. It's the same basis that much of Chronomancy is based on." Sungmin yawned, making his words a bit difficult to understand.

"Well then, we should continue on. If what ya saw was the real deal, then that means there's probably some stairs somewhere leading back out, right?" Myth gave Roanoke a smile and pet his head. "Good job."

"I didn't do anything." Roanoke sighed. "But I don't know why I saw that."

"Who knows?" Sungmin stood beside Roanoke and studied the man once more, though this time he seemed to be judging if he was okay.

With the way Roanoke was still wavering, Sungmin followed his uneasy steps carefully. Roanoke made a face as he noticed this, not wanting any sort of pity. He certainly wasn't overly comfortable with the man yet. Their exchange earlier had just been a matter of information, not conversation. Roanoke increased his steps in an awkward manner, leading the way in a much less confident march than Kaleida had.

chapter six

THE VEINS THAT THEY HAD SEEN earlier in the walls soon vanished, but along the left side of the wall, a large hole appeared. It was crafted in a perfect circle, and a set of stairs carved into the stone descended further down. A plaque hung above the hole, but time had rusted away the words that might have been on it. On the side, there was another almost-sign with the wooden pole still rising above the ground, but whatever had been on it was nowhere in sight.

"Welllllllll? What do you think, Roan? Was I right, or was I right? This has gotta be a lead! It might even be an adventure." Kaleida nudged her brother with one arm.

Roanoke knew what she was after and wasn't about to give it to her, though the corners of his mouth twitched with a smile.

"Your instincts have come through... this one time," he said with measured words.

"Aw, come on. Give me more credit than that."

"Nope. Don't want your head getting any bigger than it already is." With a smirk, Roanoke flicked Kaleida's hat and nearly knocked it off in the process. Kaleida made a face and gave him a light push back.

"Dick." She adjusted her hat back to its proper spot.

"Those stairs are goin' down, though. That can't be the stairs that Roan's ghost friends were talkin' bout, right?" Myth pouted.

"It's an odd setup." Sungmin had walked up to the entry and looked at the plaque on top, then turned his attention back to Roanoke. "You were reading about this place, weren't you? Did you find anything about what this might be?"

"Nothing." Roanoke glanced at Sungmin and then looked away. He felt himself tensing up once more, wishing that he had some piece of information that he could give so that he didn't feel so lost and stupid. "There's not a lot of information about this asteroid. It's too small."

"Oh well." Sungmin looked away, leaving it at that. As he did, Roanoke frowned and walked up to the entrance.

"This might have something to do with whatever those workers were building, though. It might be worth checking out." A shiver ran down Roanoke's body as he felt something rush by him, through him, from within. Perhaps it was the same strange wind that had saved them, the one that everyone had seemed to conveniently forget about. But there was more that called to him from within. He closed his eyes, and he could almost hear a faint tune that came from within the darkness. A familiar song.

The moment was interrupted by the music from Sungmin's headphones. Roanoke opened his eyes to see the musician had stepped past him to examine the wall just inside the entrance. Sungmin beckoned Roanoke over without looking at him, and he hesitated a moment before obeying.

"Look at this. Sort of odd, don't you think?" Sungmin pointed to a small plaque on the interior, then wiped it clean with one of his thick sleeves. Roanoke squinted his eyes, and the Insta-Light orb hovered closer to provide enough lighting for him to finally make out the words on it.

"Watch your step?" Roanoke read the words out loud, his voice lifting slightly with confusion.

"I don't usually see deep dark caves with warning signs." Kaleida barreled past Roanoke to stand between him and Sungmin. "How nice of them."

He stumbled back as he was shoved but found himself caught by Myth. The wyvernboy sympathetically righted Roanoke and offered him a smile.

"Guess we're goin' all out on this compass search, eh?" he joked quietly with Roanoke, though he looked a little sheepish and hesitant as well.

"Come on, Roan!" Kaleida turned and grabbed her brother's arm in much the same way that she had done with Sungmin, tugging him towards the staircase. "I need your light, and you've still gotta do some groveling to me for being right."

ROANOKE was helpless in Kaleida's grasp, giving Myth and Sungmin a pleading look as he was tugged into the darkness. Myth gave another laugh, leaving the poor man to his fate. He was about to start down the stairs as well when he noticed that Sungmin had not moved from his place on the first step.

It was the first time Myth had really looked at their new recruit. The way Sungmin's expression felt so empty, and his eyes so emotionless, was unnerving to the wyvernboy. He was used to being around the twins, who had the worst time keeping their emotions in check. Even Roanoke was brutally blunt and honest with his emotions when he finally let them out in bursts.

"Sorry to drag ya into this mess," Myth said in the most conversational tone that he could manage.

"He seems scared of me." Sungmin murmured, as though he were saying it to himself.

Myth followed his gaze, looking at Roanoke's back as the man was attempting to break free from his sister's tight hold.

"Who, Roan? Naw, he's just a bit anxious around strangers. He's got a rough tongue, but he don't usually mean any harm by it. You'll get used to him soon enough."

"He's honest, in his own way. You all are. It's... strange." His voice, drifting in and out like the tide, felt just as cool and peaceful as the waves. Myth couldn't help but stare at the man a little more, taking in his words.

"You ever been on a team? Because a good one's like that."

Sungmin finally tore his gaze away from the tunnel to look at Myth. He smiled at the man, but it was hollow and held no joy or bitterness, no emotion at all.

"I'm not much of a team person."

THE group descended the stairs without much flair, their trip assisted by the strange and unnecessary arrows that had been drawn on the sides of the walls. While Kaleida seemed happy to chalk it up to past adventurers leaving helpful clues, the rest of the group were a little more suspicious about it. None of them had a reasonable explanation for it, however, and it didn't seem like leaving arrows was an inherently malevolent thing to do. So, accepting the arrows pointing in the only direction to go, the group walked down to the last step.

A large and mostly empty room greeted them. The space seemed intentionally made, like the stairway. The walls had been smoothed down, and large stone pillars with basic designs were raised periodically in the room, though they did not actually reach the ceiling. The most striking thing about the room was the set of large knight statues that formed a straight line. There were three on each side, and two in the center. The figures stretched up to the ceiling like the pillars, though they did not quite reach as high. The knights held various heavy stone weaponry in their hands, but otherwise were relatively basic and simple compared to the more intricate pillars. Past them, a large entryway leading off into darkness stood directly across from the group.

"See? Doesn't this just scream adventure?" Kaleida laughed. She took in a deep breath, but coughed a little on the dust that drifted in the room.

"It screams something, that's for sure." Roanoke wandered a little further in, studying the pillars and knights. "I don't understand, though. Why would the Wayfinder's Compass—"

As Myth and Sungmin approached, Roanoke cut himself short. He wasn't entirely certain why; perhaps it was lingering self-consciousness about his comparative lack of knowledge. Perhaps it was still the distrust of the strange and aloof new recruit, though that had been made somewhat difficult due to his sister's blabbing about their goal. Sungmin hadn't even commented much on the Wayfinder's Compass or their search for it.

Why not say something...? Ugh. Trying to piece it together made Roanoke's head hurt. "The air in here is charged with Stardust energy," Sungmin murmured, as though sensing that the last thing Roanoke needed at that moment was him spewing more observations.

I could sense that, Roanoke thought bitterly.

"Hm... I thought it felt a bit different in here." Kaleida looked at her watch and picked out an app that functioned as a Stardust detector. As she held it up, the group could see it scan the room with a thin green light. Once done, the scanner projected a general sense of Stardust, and eight distinct orbs of concentrated energy matched the eight knights in the room.

"That's... not super surprising." Kaleida sighed, a bit of wind taken out of her sails. She took a few steps forward and squinted as she examined the knights. "They're covered in dust, though. Maybe they're just really big magic magnets? We could probably speed through here, honestly."

"I don't know if that's a good idea, Kal. It seems like there's a trap set up." Roanoke walked forward to stand next to his over-eager sister.

He turned his gaze towards the knights as well. As his sister had said, they were covered in dust. There seemed to be something off about them, however. As he studied them, he noted how their chests all seemed to be emblazoned with the same design. An arrow and something that he couldn't make out.... It was was strangely familiar to him, though he couldn't quite place where he had seen it before.

"Traps," Myth scoffed, putting his hands on his hips. "The lazy man's weapon."

"Hm, is that so? I should learn how to use them, then." Sungmin smiled, a reaction that Roanoke caught and frowned at.

"Either way, we should move carefully—"

Roanoke's words were interrupted by a shattering sound,. The force of it caused the three to shake as the earth they were standing on became briefly unstable.

Ahead of them, Kaleida had run forward. Her spirit and gut and a bad lack of common sense had left her stuck on her speedrun idea. But, as she got near the last of the knights, the axe that it wielded slammed down into the floor just in front of her. The young woman barely had enough time to jump back and make a face at the interruption.

"...Well, there were bound to be traps." Kaleida glanced back at the others and offered them a sheepish grin.

"You're too casual about this!" Roanoke took a few more steps forward to try and reach his sister, but as he did so, the other knights creaked and groaned as they came to life. With loud metallic sounds, they began moving towards Kaleida and the group.

Kaleida's eyes practically sparkled, and Roanoke couldn't hide his own interest at the incoming fight. He knew Kaleida would be getting them into some kind of trouble today, and the fight before them was too interesting to resist. Still, he kept his expression as disapproving as possible for Kaleida's sake.

"You're too serious! Come on, Roan! This is our chance to show our new team member what we can do!" Kaleida laughed.

She opened her inventory screen and withdrew her trusty rifle, an old and rusty thing that had colorful accents drawn into the barrel of the gun. From the belt around her hips, she took out several papers that had been fashioned into what looked like bullets—and, for Kaleida, they were.

Putting them in the gun, she pointed it at one of the knights and smirked. "Watch closely, Sungmin! Let's have fun with this."

"This isn't a show!" Roanoke groaned.

In spite of his words, however, he focused for the upcoming fight. He stretched one hand out, and below it, a long katana formed into existence in a burst of Stardust. The weapon was silver and accented with the same rainbow markings that were on Kaleida's rifle. With an exhale, he lunged.

He needed height to be able to do any actual damage to these golems. They were slow and awkward, but Roanoke was fairly certain just going for their knees to topple them wouldn't work the same as it normally would with beasts, abominations, and the like.

"Kal! Stairs, now!" he called out.

Kaleida pointed her rifle at the ground. She fired once and the force of it propelled her upwards. She threw paper down and they formed platforms to hover on. Landing on one of them, she aimed her rifle at one of the knight's heads and fired. The bullet shot into the stone helmet and sent the creature falling backward.

Roanoke took advantage of the platforms his sister had created. He leaped from platform to platform until he could get to a knight of his own, barely dodging a sword that was bigger than he was in the process. Once he was high enough, Roanoke couldn't help but grin slightly. He jumped onto a knight and slashed his katana across the thing's throat, then ran across its shoulders and jumped to another knight as the first golem's hands reached up to grab at him.

Myth, meanwhile, had taken a few steps back as two of the golems approached him and Sungmin. He glanced back at the grey-haired man, who merely gave him a shrug in return. With a long sigh, Myth took out his deck of cards and grinned at the creatures.

"Today just ain't your lucky day," he said in a stylish fashion, tipping his hat.

His deck glowed before him, and the first five cards in the deck shot out and spun in a circle in front of him. His golden-brown eyes scanned the cards quickly. As they began to return to the deck, he snatched one. Holding it up so the golems could see, Myth chuckled.

"It really ain't your day."

The card was an eight of spades. It hardly looked like anything impressive but, as Myth flung it expertly at the first golem, the card burst into eight large and obsidian-like spades that shot through the golem. It shattered the creature on impact, and stone bits fell onto the floor.

"Guess I had the better hand." Myth smirked and struck another pose.

"Pay attention!" Kaleida fired a few more paper bullets at her knight.

She scaled further up on the paper platforms, which were beginning to fall apart with her own lack of focus. She leaped onto the head of her knight and positioned her rifle onto the top of its head.

"Paper beats rock, asshole!" she snapped and, with a grin, fired three rounds through the top of the golem's head. For a moment, the golem simply wavered, then large paper spikes shot out from the interior of its' body. Like Myth's target, the golem crumbled. As she fell, Kaleida quickly reloaded her rifle and shot at the ground once more, allowing her to regain her footing and land on the same knight as her brother.

"Get yourself another one, Kal." Roanoke dug his katana deeper into the neck of the golem. He grunted as the weapon wouldn't cut all the way through, and felt himself blush as the group's eyes fell on him.

"Roan, you could use—" A look from Roanoke silenced her and Kaleida merely rolled her eyes. She created a bridge of paper and ran off to the third golem.

"I got this."

Roanoke tried to think of an alternative, but the golem's hand rose up and grabbed him. He cried out as he felt his body crushed by the heavy hand, squirming as he tried to get out. It seemed, in fact, that he did not have this. He had one free hand, which he used to create a dagger. He stabbed it desperately into the hand, but it had less effect than the katana.

"Roan! I'm coming, buddy!" Myth rushed forward as he heard his friend cry out. The wyvernboy glanced back at Sungmin. "You got that big guy, right?" Myth called out, motioning to the second golem that had been heading towards them.

Before waiting for an answer, Myth was gone. He ducked and slid past the stone rubble and moving legs of the surviving golems until he slid in front of the one holding onto Roanoke.

"Hold on!" Myth called out.

"I can't exactly do anything else!" Roanoke snapped back at Myth.

He decided to change his tactics. Letting the dagger drop to the ground, Roanoke created a staff with a spade end, and he tried to wedge it between himself and the hand holding him.

"A'right, enough with the sass..." Myth grumbled.

Roanoke watched him take a moment to consider his next move. Myth's luck Stardust allowed him to see the top five cards in his deck and select one, though the rest were reshuffled after. The wyvernboy took a deep breath and drew the top card.

Myth looked down at it, and Roanoke could instantly tell he didn't get the one he wanted.

Five of hearts.

"Hey buddy, how much of a handle do ya have on the situation? Like, do ya think you could wiggle your body out any time soon?" Myth gave Roanoke an apologetic look.

"Fuck!" Roanoke retorted.

He sucked in his breath as he felt the hand holding him suddenly whirl, aiming to slam him into the wall. He closed his eyes, bracing himself for what was sure to be a knock-out level impact. Rather than the pain and sound of rock shattering, however, he felt the hand jerk back with a BOING! sound. He opened his eyes to see a giant heart-shaped pillow against the wall, and four more heart-shaped pillows floating around the space. He couldn't help but give Myth a dry look, and the wyvernboy shrugged.

"It helped, didn't it!?" he yelled.

Roanoke took the brief pause to survey the rest of the scene. Kaleida, for her part, had taken down the golem that she had landed on with more of her paper bullets. As the golem crumbled, she jumped down to the floor. She too watched the rest of the battle; there were three more left. And Sungmin...

Kaleida and Roanoke blinked as they looked in his direction. The golem that was just a moment ago heading his way was in pieces around him. The young man hadn't seemed to move at all and merely gave a yawn before meeting Kaleida's gaze. Roanoke was unable to stop his frown. Kaleida seemed to ignore her own confusion and ran after the one remaining golem. Roanoke exhaled. As long as she didn't use much paper or energy, she could—

A swing of a club into the earth came too close to Kaleida. Before she could dodge, rocks and force hit her and sent her flying back. She landed in a crumpled heap on the earth and laid there for a moment, trying to regain her senses.

"Damn it..." Kaleida winced as she struggled to sit up.

"Kal!" Roanoke's eyes widened as he saw her, and he began struggling more. "Myth, go help her! Fucking forget about me!"

Myth looked reluctant but gave a nod. "I got ya, Kal!"

Myth moved in her direction. By the time he got to her side, the golem had raised a club over their heads. Myth took a deep breath, looking hopeful once more. With a firm nod, he drew out the next card.

Three of diamonds. Not a total loss, but it wasn't a show-stopper. With a huff, Myth flung the card. Following the path the card flew, three large and jagged spikes shot up from the ground. The golem staggered as it tripped and fell onto the spikes. It wasn't quite enough to destroy it, however, and it reached out a shaky hand at the pair.

In the blink of an eye, there was a perfect hole in the golem's head. There had been no sound, no cue it had happened. But as the hole appeared, black veins came from the wound and quickly spread throughout the golem's body. The golem collapsed into tiny pieces, the parts covered in veins crumbling away into ash.

"What the Tartarus..." Myth looked in Sungmin's direction.

Sungmin blinked as they looked at him, and gave one more shrug. His gaze, however, drifted over to Roanoke. He closed his red eyes for a moment.

"Sungmin?" Kaleida called out to him, appearing unsure whether to be concerned or angry that the man's response was so subdued.

Sungmin didn't respond, instead opening an app on his watch. He tapped a few buttons on it, and it was clear soon enough that he had disconnected his headphones from the Chroniker. Music began to blast throughout the space, but Kaleida only frowned further. It wasn't music he created, so it wasn't a Stardust ability, but—

Roanoke's eyes widened as he realized what Sungmin was doing–and Kaleida gasped as she figured it out, too.

"W-wait! Sungmin, you don't want to do that!" She quickly looked at her brother with concern.

As the song reached Roanoke's ears, he shook. There was no way the man could have known, right? Roanoke couldn't think, however; his Prismatic Core center began to glow with power. Their luminescence throbbed in time to the beat of the music, absorbing it and filling Roanoke. The song entered his soul and coursed through his body, and he felt himself pulsing with power. It was an urgent and aggressive song, filled with fury and crashing like a tidal wave.

Roanoke's eyes glowed with newfound ability and he turned his glare to the golem. The weapon in his hand turned into a trident and, with a scream, he pointed it at the golem's head. As though responding to the song, a tsunami-force blast of water shot out from the trident and severed the head he had tried to cut previously from its body. The golem's head flew off into the distance, slamming against one wall before falling to pieces. Roanoke was just able to crawl out from the hand as the body fell. As he began falling too, Myth rushed over and held out his hands.

"Land in my arms, buddy! Right here!!" he called out to Roanoke, arms wide open for the catch. Roanoke, who had no control over where he fell, looked down at Myth.

"Move, you stupid-!"

He fell on top of Myth's head; the man was just a little off in his position. The pair collapsed to the floor, leaving Sungmin as the only one standing.

"I'M just saying, that could have gone worse." Kaleida nursed one of the Health Ups that Roanoke had brought.

Roanoke, on the other hand, was sipping at a Diet HP with an expression of annoyance. His hard gaze was on Sungmin. The grey-haired man had reconfigured his headphones back to his watch and was relaxing as he listened to the music.

"I'm surprised the pillow card helped," Myth said, a little bit of triumph echoing in his voice. Each of them had grabbed one of the heart pillows to rest on as they healed up.

"First time for everything, I guess." Kaleida smiled and started alternating between downing the health potion and chugging Stardust energy shots. Roanoke made a face at his sister.

"That can't taste good," he muttered dryly.

Kaleida stuck her tongue out at him. "Better than your cooking, though."

She laughed, and he couldn't help but relax a bit despite the fact that she had just insulted him. His gaze went back to Sungmin and he frowned once more, though this time it was a bit tamer.

"Did you know about that?" he asked, voice a little faint.

"About what?" Sungmin replied, eyes closed and hands resting on his chest. "By the way, these pillows are great. A+ ability."

"Well thank ya-" Myth puffed up his chest.

"About the music. Me and music," Roanoke said over Myth, knowing the man would begin to ramble on if he let him.

Sungmin said nothing at first, keeping his eyes closed and body relaxed. After a moment, he whispered, "That gauntlet is a Teien artifact, isn't it?"

Roanoke turned his gaze down to his fetter and the gemstone embedded in it. "Yeah. But how-"

"Teien artifacts usually have Prismatic Ore Cores. That has one." Sungmin curled up a little more in the pillow.

"Promise you won't tell anyone about them? Not everyone knows what a Teien artifact looks like, and it'd cause a lot of trouble for Roan if people found out he had one..." Kaleida pouted, taking a pause from her double shots. She brought a hand to the rainbow goggles around her neck, giving them a slight wave. "I have one too, but I don't use them like Roan does so a lot of people just think they're... you know, decorative? But if people found out, they'd—"

"They'd try and take them from you. I know. You don't have to worry." Sungmin half-opened his eyes, looking at the twins with a dull smile. As he did, Roanoke couldn't help but notice the way the man's eyes seemed a little paler, though it was difficult to say for certain since they weren't open fully.

"You didn't answer my question." Roanoke turned his gaze down to his Diet HP drink, swirling the remaining liquid at the bottom of the can and watching the bright pink mini whirlpool that formed. "Did you know about the music? And me?"

"You mean the fact that your powers are affected by music?" Sungmin said off-handedly, closing his eyes once more. "I had a feeling."

Kaleida sat up a little more, but it was clear that some of her excitement had wavered and a bit more concern had entered into her voice. "That's another thing we'd like you not to mention to other people..."

Roanoke bit his lip at Kaleida's words. His gaze was hard as he swirled his drink even harder for a moment before downing it. "And don't play music around me again, got it?" he growled.

Kaleida shook her head. "You know that's not going to help, Roan. If you're going to learn to control it, then you need to-"

"I don't need to do anything. I'm fine as I am." Roanoke stood up and crushed the can before opening his inventory screen and tapping the trash icon. A small black hole appeared, and Roanoke tossed the can into it before closing it out. Without saying a word further, he began to walk on towards the entry into the next room.

KALEIDA sighed, watching Roanoke head off. "He's just antsy." She paused and considered something before facing Sungmin once more. "Sungmin, did you know what effect that song would have on him? Or what he could do with his artifact?"

"I had a feeling." Sungmin began to stand up, cracking his back as he did so.

"You got a lot of feelings, friend," Myth said dryly, watching Sungmin with a raised eyebrow.

"Do I? I hadn't noticed." Sungmin seemed to genuinely consider it. He adjusted his guitar case back on his body and started to walk forward.

"Wait!" Kaleida rushed up to Sungmin and grabbed his arm. "Sungmin, if you knew what he could do with that song, then... Do you think you would know what he could do with others? Like, if you were to play different songs, could you tell what they would do to him?"

Sungmin paused and stared down at Kaleida. His expression was carefully guarded even as he wore a faint smile. "...I think so, yes."

"Then help him! I won't ask how you know... I don't even care, as long as it helps my brother. He's scared of his own power." Kaleida turned her gaze downward to hide the sadness in her eyes. "Songs are unpredictable. You never know what a new one might do to you. How it makes you feel. With Roanoke, the abilities he gets and the weapon he wields can change if there's a song playing around him... That's his artifact's power. It absorbs the music and sounds around him and changes it into something. But unless he's heard the song before, he won't know what he can do.... Or what it can do to him. It's dangerous for everyone, and back then..."

"The short version is, if you know how he's gonna be with the song, then you're in the best place to get him back into the swing of things." Myth gave Kaleida a nudge before offering Sungmin a grin. "Think you can help out with that? He'll fight you over it at first, but I think he's starting to cool down around ya."

Sungmin appraised the two silently. Finally, he gave a small nod of his head.

"I'll do what I can."

chapter seven

"DID YOU SEE THAT?"

In the wreckage of the stone golems, golden feathers danced. The tell-tale shimmer wavered over one part of the room, then dispersed to reveal the two figures who had first saved the group. The one who had spoken was the shorter, more energetic one. They were seated on one of the stone helmets, little legs kicking back and forth idly.

"That was crazy, right? Don't you think it was crazy?"

The taller figure furrowed his brow, fanning himself as he walked about and looked at the pieces. "It was something."

The peacock man found one of the heart-shaped bed-sized pillows and plopped into it. As he got himself comfortable, he watched his companion.

"I can't believe those twins had Teien artifacts. And did you see that other guy?"

"Yes, I saw the exact same things you did. We were standing right next to each other." The peacock man gave a dramatic sigh, resting his head in one hand. "They were a complete and utter mess, weren't they? I was starting to feel like I was going to have to step in again. Pitiful."

"I guess, but that sleepy guy sure was something. When he took down that golem, that power he used..." The shorter figure stopped. "... Do you think he's one of *them*?"

"It's irrelevant, isn't it? We're here to find the compass before Kani does. That's all." The figure stood up from the pillow, though he had some trouble doing so given how much the comfortable seat had sucked him in. With a grunt, he managed to pull himself up somewhat ungracefully.

The shorter figure gave a sigh and hopped down. They ran to catch up with their friend. "I guess. But if they need help... Like, really need it, then we're going to help them again, right, Maymay?"

The peacock stopped and bit his lip.

"They really are a mess, aren't they?"

"PUZZLE. it's definitely a puzzle." Kaleida said firmly, her arms crossed over her chest as she examined the room that they had just entered.

Like the other, it was a large and open space. However, there were periodic gaps in the walls. They were curiously set, the space within like a mini cave. As Roanoke looked around, he mused at how they looked like booths. Additionally, though the room was mostly empty, the center of it was filled with stone circles that rose out of the ground several feet in the air.

"But the exit's right over there. Doesn't even have doors or locks or anythin'." Myth surveyed the room, hands on his hips.

"In my experience-"

"Video game experience," Roanoke sassed, flashing Kaleida a smirk.

"I still have more dungeon experience than YOU," Kaleida retorted, her eyes narrowing.

"Ya know..." Myth said slowly, a smile starting to rise on his features as he developed a fantastic idea. "It could be that the floor's lava, and ya gotta jump from circle to circle?"

"Oh yeah, the perfect dungeon riddle for children," Kaleida snorted. "Look, there's gotta be something around here that tells us what to do. Roan, start searching!"

"Why am I in charge of searching?" Roanoke sighed. Absently, he twirled his braid around one finger as he began to move into the room. Despite the foolishness of Myth's idea, he couldn't help but suck in his breath a little when he took the first real step into the room... just in case.

When the step forward brought no explosion, poison, wires, or screams, Roanoke exhaled. He made his way over to one of the gaps in the wall. A small plaque on one side of it caught his attention. It had been faded with time and covered with a layer of dust, but he brought his sleeve up and wiped at it. Though difficult to make out, there were words listed on the plaque: *Candied Shawcraberries... Hard Health Seltzers... Mocha Manas with Caramel Drizzles and Dragonspark Flakes.*

The food options hit Roanoke's brain like a slap to the face. He took a step back to observe the gap once more. There was a counter, and there were spaces within that had faint outlines where the wall was cleaner, like something had been pressed up against there. The young Teien spun around to stare at the circles that were jutting out from the floor. As dots connected within his brain, he opened his mouth to call out to the others.

"I think there's a trap," Sungmin shouted calmly before Roanoke could say a single word.

"Really? What kind is it?" Kaleida perked up immediately, looking in his direction from underneath the table she had been studying.

"Don't encourage her." Roanoke sighed. Having stayed the closest to Sungmin, he merely glanced over at the man disapprovingly. If the place was what he thought it was, then—

"I don't have to. They will." Sungmin motioned to the booths around them.

Large green oozes began to tumble out from the shadows. The slimes rolled towards the group, leaving a trail behind them. One could practically see the shudder that ran up Kaleida's spine as she saw them. Despite having more experience than the others in terms of dungeons, oozes were something that she didn't mess with.

"Big nope on that one." She yelped and darted towards the exit.

Before she could get too far, however, an ooze tendril shot out and wrapped around her leg. She growled as she hit the floor. She opened her inventory and drew out several more papers before sending them flying at the ooze. The slime swallowed the papers whole, ignoring how sharp and hard they were, with absolutely no impact or effect.

Kaleida paled. "Guys!?"

"Dealing with our own shit!" Roanoke snapped.

The slimes had moved towards the two as well. Myth's cards were absorbed by the oozes before they could become effects, and Roanoke found that creating a club to deal bludgeoning damage had only a moderate amount of success against the slimes.

"Anyone got an ace up their sleeves!?" Myth yelled out over the slish-slosh sounds of the fighting.

To anyone else, it might have been almost comical to watch the three squirming and fighting helplessly against what essentially looked like a bunch of green apple jelly, but the hiss of acid as the oozes brushed against their clothing revealed the true danger of the fight.

Sungmin blinked a few times and concentrated on the group. He next turned his gaze to the path that they had just come from. The cogs in his brain seemed to slowly rotate as he considered the situation. He gave the faintest of frowns but made his way over to one of the circles with his usual slow speed. The musician hopped up to sit on the table and gently pulled out his guitar. It was an old acoustic thing, with deep red paint and black strings. He placed it on one knee as he began to tune it, lost in his own little world.

As he did, a tendril shot out at Roanoke and wrapped around his arm. The young man gave a shout of pain as the acid burned at his skin, but the rainbow gem embedded on the fetter glowed with power. It gave a small burst of energy, which was enough to send the ooze back.

"Sungmin!!" Roanoke snapped, cradling his injured arm to his chest as he continued swinging the club with one hand.

The grey-haired man wasn't hurried by the other's cry. He finished tuning his guitar, then began to play. As he played and sang, a quiet descended upon the room. Even the oozes were entranced as they were drawn into the man's earnest voice and music. It swirled through the room, and Roanoke tensed as he waited for a major reaction from his fetter. He was surprised to find that, though the music worked its way deep within him as it usually did, he felt no surge of power or emotion. Instead, there was almost a peacefulness that settled within him, a soothing feeling akin to being bundled up in blankets. He couldn't help but take a deep breath and close his eyes as he reluctantly enjoyed the feeling.

The song came to an end after a few short minutes. As it did so, the silence that had filled the room persisted a moment longer. Then, with the concert over, the oozes suddenly snapped back to life and began their assault.

"I thought they were weak to Stardust!? What's the deal!?" Kaleida leaped over one of the circles as an ooze splashed dangerously close to her.

"They are. But that wasn't Stardust," Sungmin replied with a yawn in his tone. He rested his head against the guitar and watched the group as they resumed fighting.

"Why play at all, then!? Help us!!" Roanoke stumbled back as another ooze lunged at him, but this time he swung his club like he was wielding a bat and sent some of the ooze splattering against a booth.

"I am."

At Sungmin's words, a powerful gust of wind swept through the room. It struck out at the circles and booths with blade-like intensity. Sungmin got up just as one particular gust of air cut the circle he had been on in half. His frown turned slightly upwards, but he focused on putting away his guitar. As the winds lashed out, they began slicing the oozes into pieces and sending gooey chunks everywhere.

Standing at the entrance to the room were two flashy figures.

The peacock man stood at the ready, his deep purple eyes full of confidence and a smirk on his features. His fan was pointed at the oozes, while the other hand rested on his hip.

"Don't worry, Maymay, I got the rest!" the smaller figure chirped.

With a mischievous smile, they ran and took a leap. As they were in the air, their body shifted and formed into that of a hummingbird. The bird flew upwards and hovered over the remaining slimes. With another shift, they had become a mighty elephant. Their body fell through the air like a bomb, leaving Kaleida, Myth, and Roanoke to stare open-mouthed as it crushed the slimes below it and sent more of the ooze splattering against the nearby walls and booths.

With the monsters made into sample-sized gelatin, the peacock man strolled up to the group and gave a light wave with his fan. The elephant ran to the peacock's side and made a noise of greeting. At the strange arrival, the four members looked among each other before Roanoke approached, his expression cautious and body tense.

"Who are you—?"

"Say thank you," the purple-eyed man retorted, waving his fan at Roanoke and raising an eyebrow expectantly.

"Excuse me?" Roanoke stared at him in disbelief.

"You heard me. I saved your life. I expect a thank you."

"You don't just ask for a thank you."

"I'm not asking. I'm demanding."

Roanoke sputtered, an occurrence which neither Myth nor Kaleida had ever seen before. The pair exchanged mild looks of disbelief before setting their sights back on what was sure to be quite the show.

"Then I'm not saying it." Roanoke crossed his arms over his chest. His eyes were full of fire and fury, his frown tight and twitching from anger.

"Then I'm not saving you again." The peacock man huffed, snapping his fan closed in front of Roanoke's face.

"Fine. I didn't ask you to save me anyways!"

"Why you ungrateful little-"

"Guys!!" The shorter figure's voice, rather absurdly coming from the elephant's body, called out over the arguing. Unfortunately, the two men were locked into their battle.

"At least I don't have to beg people for thanks-"

"Hey? Guys!?" The plea came again, a little louder. Once more, they were ignored.

"Beg? If you want to see begging, I can make that happen—"

"GUYS!" The shorter figure finally screamed from their position in the distance.

Like synchronized clockwork, both Roanoke and the peacock man snapped their heads in the young figure's direction.

"WHAT!?" They both shouted in unison, then glared at each other for daring to harmonize.

"Is it supposed to do that?" The smaller figure pointed with their elephant snout behind the group.

As they all turned and looked, the oozes had formed together. A single massive ooze stared down at the group intimidatingly, the acid dripping from its slippery body.

chapter eight

A REAL-LIFE "..." MOMENT ECHOED throughout the room as the slime looked at them and they looked at the slime. Then, the moment broke, and the group scattered. Kaleida jumped over several of the circles, quickly trying to draw out her shotgun. Myth ran to one corner and looked at his deck, but hesitated when he saw how low the cards were getting.

Roanoke rushed back. As he moved, he saw that Sungmin was standing in the same position he had been in when the two figures had first arrived. Swearing inwardly, he grabbed the young man and dragged him back.

"Come on! Don't just stand there!" He pulled him back just as the ooze sent an acid splash attack.

The group found themselves being chased around the room by the large ooze. Though slow, it could easily close the distance between it and them. It was almost humorous, but hardly anyone could enjoy it. Even the fact that one of the runners was a large elephant didn't quite seem to lighten the mood, particularly when one acidic whip lashed a little too close for comfort.

Finally, the peacock man stopped. He stamped his foot and pointed his feathery fan at the ooze once more. The wind started to pick up around him.

"I did NOT sign up to play with ooze! Aquila! We're going with the heavy fire!"

At the declaration, the smaller figure stopped and gasped happily. "Got it, Maymay!" They practically squealed.

"Aquila...?" Roanoke muttered under his breath, furrowing his brow. The name registered in his brain, but there were other matters far more pressing than identifying what.

Aquila, as they were so recently called, turned back into a hummingbird and fluttered into the air. At the same time, the purple-eyed figure sent a whirlwind around the ooze, holding it in place.

"Right idea, wrong creature!" Aquila laughed.

High above the ooze, the bird suddenly shifted. There was a burst of light and warmth, and then the group found themselves looking at a whale. A whale that happened to be on fire. A whale on fire that happened to take up the entirety of the room. The group stared up at the new development with dizzy wonder.

"I have some concerns," Sungmin said quietly next to Roanoke, and he could only nod in response.

"Run!" Kaleida screamed, though there was excitement playing at the edges of her eyes. She grabbed Myth and ran to one of the booths, ducking behind it.

Roanoke followed her lead. He grabbed Sungmin with his uninjured arm and ducked behind another booth. As the group hid, the purple-eyed man gave a devious grin. They could hear the sound of the collision, hear the sounds of squishing and stone breaking. From where they sat hidden under the booths, they could see fiery remains of ooze hit the walls above them and continue to burn. When they finally dared to poke their heads above the booths, they saw the giant fiery whale reform back into the tiny form of Aquila. The green-eyed shapeshifter saw them and waved eagerly.

The taller figure scoffed and fanned himself once more. "Peasant," he muttered disapprovingly under his breath.

Slowly, the group approached the pair after making their way out of the booths. Kaleida was the first to reach them. She immediately went to Aquila, throwing her arms around them in a loose hug.

"That was so cool!" Kaleida gasped.

Aquila allowed the hold and laughed lightly. "The coolest, yeah! I can turn into anything I want if I've seen it once. Not going to lie, I've seen A LOT of weird animals."

"That's so incredible. And you..." Kaleida turned to face the other man, her eyes growing a little wider. "Way back then... That was you with the wind, wasn't it?"

The peacock man didn't respond. His cocky grin faded a little bit and he merely glanced away with a huff. As he did so, however, he noticed Roanoke approaching him. One could practically see his feathers preening as he prepared for another battle. Instead, Roanoke held out his uninjured hand. He didn't dare to look the man in the eye, staring instead at the ground to hide the blush on his features.

"...Thank you." Roanoke's voice was so quiet that it was easy to miss.

"Excuse me?" The peacock man grinned, leaning down a little.

"I'm only saying it once."

The peacock man opened his mouth to retort but, as he looked at Roanoke, he noted the way that the other cradled his injured arm to his chest.

"Don't thank me," he said, his tone surprisingly serious.

"What? You give me all kinds of shit for not thanking you before, and now you—"

"You're injured. I didn't protect you." His gaze hardened and he brought one hand out, grabbing the other's injured arm.

"Fuck! Hey, what are you—" Roanoke hissed with pain, confusion, and anger.

He looked ready to slam his uninjured fist into the man's face, but he paused as he saw the other's eyes glow. Golden feathers fell over the injured arm and, after a few moments, the injury was healed. As soon as the peacock let go, Roanoke retracted his arm and looked him over. The purple-eyed man didn't speak, but looked away in the same blushing manner that Roanoke had.

An awkward silence emerged as the exchange finished. Kaleida, still hugging Aquila loosely, watched her brother closely as she tried to gauge his reaction. Roanoke couldn't decide his reaction at all, and Myth seemed relatively puzzled about the fact that two people had just randomly shown up to save them. Sungmin was the one to step forward, tilting his head in the peacock and Aquila's directions.

"Was that healing Stardust?" he asked gently, nodding his head at the purple-eyed man. The latter made a face.

"Stardust? It was just magic."

"Stardust is the more specific term for magic—" Sungmin began to explain, but was interrupted by a heavy sigh from the taller man.

"Everything is so annoyingly specific in this day and age. Whatever happened to vague titles with little explanation? I liked that."

Roanoke furrowed his brow, turning his attention from his healed arm to the taller man. "... This age?"

"You called them Aquila earlier. And that shapeshifting ability... It seems very familiar to the CoS known as Aquila." Sungmin tilted his head at the pair, expression neutral but eyes questioning.

The peacock man and Aquila both jumped. Inwardly, Roanoke could also feel himself startling from the observation. The familiarity he had felt before in regards to Aquila's name... That must have been it. While he had some of the names memorized, others like Aquila were less well known. He stared hard at the shorter figure, trying to size them up. Very few pictures existed of Aquila, or any of the CoS, which made it difficult to identify them. But Aquila, the Dynamic Roc, was known for their shapeshifting ability, and—

"Did I say Aquila? Sorry, sometimes I butcher my friend's names. Their name is... Aki," the peacock man said quickly. "And I'm... Maymay."

"You sound very confident in your names," Sungmin mused quietly.

"What are you two doing here, anyway?" Roanoke muttered.

He massaged his healed arm, trying his best to appraise them. There was no way that the small green-eyed shapeshifter who had been called Aquila could be anything but the CoS. And the one beside him... Roanoke bit his lip. The whole reason they were after the stupid compass in the first place was to catch one of those living weapons. The possibility that two of them were just standing in front of them right now was almost ridiculous.

"We're just... uh..."

"Spelunkers!" Aquila, now Aki, said quickly, with a badly lying smile.

"Right. Spelunkers. We see a hole and we just have to jump into it and... spelunk," Maymay said slowly, furrowing his brow as he listened to his own words.

"We saw you fall down here and we knew you weren't spelunkers. Didn't have the look at all."

"Nope, don't have the look."

"But you helped us when we were falling, right? That was you guys?" Kaleida interjected. Her eyes were sparkling with the beginnings of another bad idea, and Roanoke felt a part of himself dying.

"Uh, yeah. I mean, I suppose." Maymay blushed and idly began playing with his hair. "Well, it wasn't like I was about to let a bunch of blood splatters get on me."

"Nice. Real nice." Roanoke snorted, unable to help but glare at the peacock man's choice of words.

"Be glad I don't demand a thank you for that one." Maymay smirked at Roanoke, giving him a playful wink that made Roanoke growl.

"So that's twice you saved us, huh? You know what that means..." Kaleida said slowly, her eyes practically shining like ship headlights. Roanoke and Myth both understood immediately, and both shook their heads.

"Kal, really now, we don't need-"

"We're fine as we are, I don't want-"

"I'm sure they got better things to be doin'-"

Kaleida pushed past the protests and walked up to Maymay and Aki. She clapped her hands together and took a deep breath, obviously working up to her proposal.

"Will you two join our party?"

"Kaleida!" Roanoke snapped, giving her a disapproving look. He knew what Kaleida was doing. He knew what she wanted to do. There were just too many people, however. It was too much. "We don't need more people! Sungmin doesn't even do anything as it is!" The words were tumbling out of his mouth before he could really think of them. The anxiety of the thought of more people being around was causing his heart to pound so loudly that it stifled his hearing.

"Roan, that's not fair! He took down one of those golems!"

"Did you see him do that? And what about this fight, huh? All he did was play his guitar!" Roanoke turned to face Sungmin, expression hard. "What can you do?"

"I can nap." Sungmin shrugged, his expression as unflinching as ever as he stared back at Roanoke.

"Besides that."

"I can play music."

"What else!?"

Sungmin fell silent. There was a long pause, then Roanoke shook his head and turned away.

"If you can't do anything, you shouldn't be on a team. You'll just hold everyone else back," he whispered with a shaky voice.

"Get over yourself, Roan," Kaleida snapped at her brother.

Roanoke flinched at that; his sister almost never yelled at him. He raised his head to look at her with mild surprise. Her frustrated expression sent a stab through his heart. It was one thing for him to be disapproving of Kaleida's words or actions. But to see that kind of response from her was so unusual that it almost made Roanoke apologize right out. Truthfully, some part of him was already feeling bad for how harsh he had been. Unable to sort his feelings out, he simply moved away. Roanoke groaned out loud, not even caring that everyone would be able to hear him. He turned away and put his head in his hands.

Deep breaths, he told himself, as he had done many times before.

KALEIDA looked back at Sungmin as Roanoke departed, a frown replacing her angered look. "I'm sorry about him, Sungmin. Really. You're not—"

"No, he's right," Sungmin said quickly. He offered Kaleida a small smile that was without joy, then gave a slight nod and walked off to wait near the exit.

While he walked away, Kaleida turned to both Aki and Maymay. Her expression was a mix of hope, desperation, and fear. Myth had gone off to examine the ooze remains and avoid the awkward tension, and it left her alone at the mercy of the two potential recruits.

"I'm really sorry about him. But I do think that you guys would be great on the team! You helped us twice now, and we could use some healing ability. We're running low on healing potions, and Stardust boosters, and... and, well, I really think you should join! So please..." Kaleida took a deep breath and clasped her hands together once more, apparently more willing than her brother to beg, "Please, join our team?"

"Your team? And what does your team happen to be doing down here?" Maymay gave a snort and a flip of his hair.

"We're looking for a compass," Kaleida said firmly, puffing her chest up.

"They sell those at that dirty little store-"

"Not just any compass. We're looking for the Wayfinder's Compass. It's--"

"A compass that can lead one to any of the Children of Stardust. We know." The peacock huffed and turned his attention back to the rest of the group. He seemed to be considering the situation, sharp purple eyes judging every person that moved about the room.

"Good. I can spare the exposition, then." Kaleida, unbothered by Maymay's lack of attention, stepped up closer to him. "We need all the help we can get right now. We're stuck down here, and there's nothing saying that it's down here for sure, but--"

"But?" Aki leaned in towards Kaleida. Their sparkling green eyes seemed to practically glow with excitement.

"But I feel it in my gut! And you can ask Myth or Roan, but my gut is almost never wrong. Especially not about stuff like this. It's like... a call. I know where I need to go. I'm sure Roan hears it too. But if it's just him, me, Myth, and Sungmin, we're never going to be able to get there. We can't even get out of this abyss without help."

"If you're struggling just to get out of a hole in the ground, what makes you think you can handle finding one of the CoS? The strongest weapons in the world, the God-Killers, the most wanted criminals, the... Gods, it's tiring just to list out the titles. Why even bother finding one?" Maymay muttered, but the tone in his voice suggested he was still distracted.

"And what about your brother? Are you sure he'll let us?" Aki pondered, tilting their head to watch Roanoke's tense figure. "He won't eat us or something?"

"No! He'll get used to you! He's just rough around strangers. But you—" Kaleida looked at Maymay, smiling just a little. "You challenge him! He got so worked up just talking to you! He usually can't talk like that with people. He gets so anxious he just shuts down or walks off. But he stayed to fight you! I think you'll be good for him." She seemed intent on avoiding Maymay's first question, something that the man picked up on as he turned his attention back to her.

Maymay raised an eyebrow, crossing his arms lightly over his exposed chest. "So you want me to join your team so I can annoy your brother? I must admit that it's a tempting offer."

"Yes! So you'll do it?"

"Hey! There's some more coins over here! And some random items!!" Myth's voice shouted out from the entryway. "Those oozes had some real nice stuff in them!"

"I'm in! Maymay and I are so broke!" Aki squealed. They reached out and took Kaleida's hand a firm shake, then ran off to join Myth in the coin collecting. Maymay watched his companion leave him, then sighed.

"I suppose that we've been drafted," he relented.

"Yes! You won't regret it! When we all get out of here, you'll have to come have dinner on our ship. Promise?" Kaleida grinned brightly, her expression the same as it always was when she got her way.

"I don't make promises. But we'll see." Maymay chuckled, then walked off to join his friend.

As Kaleida was left alone, her grin faded. She tapped on her watch and stared at her health, then her Stardust levels. Just looking at them made her wince a bit. They really were starting to run tight on supplies. She knew that Myth would be hurting for cards and Stardust, too. It would be hard to manage if they encountered any more fights. But now that they had two extra fighters... Kaleida sucked in her breath and forced her happy smile back in place. They would be alright. That was what a team was for, right?

Besides, the earlier conversation about Aquila versus Aki hadn't been lost on Kaleida. If there was even a slim chance that the two were CoS, wouldn't it be better for her and her group to keep them close? The others had been distracted by her twin's outburst, which left the questions about Aki's and Maymay's explanations on the sidelines. She wasn't about to throw away a good chance at support like her brother would.

That other guy, Sungmin, seemed to have more to him too. While she didn't know exactly what, his apparent musical knowledge and skill was a perfect compliment to Roanoke's unchecked abilities. Besides, there was something about him that threw her off. He was familiar to her, even though she was one hundred percent certain that she hadn't met him before. At least, maybe ninety-nine percent.

Kaleida exhaled and ran a hand through her straight hair, pulling it back briefly before letting it fall to frame her face once more. She knew that she was quick to recruit. Too quick, as her brother and Myth would agree. Kaleida had been raised by the P-300 leader. She had been raised in dungeons and had grown up alongside adventuring parties all of her life. Kaleida knew better than them that, sometimes, the universe would throw people together like this for some grand adventure. Even if her gut was entirely wrong, she had to believe in that. She was finally starting to feel like an adventurer again.

chapter nine

PAST THE BATTLE OF GOO-FILLED horror, a group of women who had missed the battle were at work in a room filled with piles of gold, gemstones, weapons, and other items that one would expect from a treasure room at the end of a dungeon. Lanterns dotted around the room in a satisfyingly atmospheric fashion, providing soft illumination and giving the gold coins an enticing glitter. It seemed, however, that the women weren't concerned with the mountain of treasures. Instead, they were hard at work on other matters. At least, some of them were, and some of them *felt* like they were.

"C'mon, Aster. How long does it take to set up a broadcaster? This usually takes you, what, like a minute? You're losing your touch, babe," one woman whined.

She stood lazily by a pile of obnoxiously tempting gold, leaning heavily on a spiked bat. In one hand, she idly tossed and caught one of the red gemstones that were scattered about. She was somewhat androgynous in appearance, wearing a pair of brown dress-pants, a bright yellow button-down shirt, and a lime green vest. Her hair, blonde and streaked with green, had been slicked back out of her features in a style that made one think of drunken businessmen about to spend a night of disappointment flirting at a hotel bar. Despite the loud and rather obnoxious outfit, her green eyes were keen, and even her lazy smile and pose couldn't fully hide the aura of a fighter.

The one she had spoken to had, some time ago, made the decision to ignore just about everything she had said. She was a short woman, a pair of large oval glasses hiding her eyes due to the shine from the lights around the room. She wore a heavy sweater and long pleated skirt. Her dull brown hair fell to split ends and the edges of her bangs suggested she nibbled on them from time to time. There was, essentially, nothing striking about the woman at all.

Still, she was dedicated to her work. She had spent a good amount of time setting up several transmitter cores, both in the room and along the path that they had taken to get down there. She would have liked to explain to her companion the sheer amount of work it took just to be able to get a signal down there, not to mention then using that weak signal to be able to broadcast back live feed to a WHOLE STAR of people, but her comrade had trouble enough managing her Chroniker watch. So, instead, Aster remained silent and focused as she finished her work.

The broadcaster, shaped like a large eye, blinked to life on the gold pile and rose into the air. As Aster looked into the eye, she could see the shimmer of electrical components made more powerful by

Stardust. She tapped an application on her watch and squinted as the streaming app showed the room and her looking down at the app.

"Ooh, meta." The bat-wielding woman behind her snorted, leaning in just enough to peer over the smaller woman's shoulder.

"We're ready to record. Nuwa, have you sensed any disturbances in the area? The connection is threadbare as it is. I do not wish for any unexpected natural developments to displace my work," Aster said, voice dull and almost mechanical as she turned towards the third figure in the room.

Sitting on the floor in front of one of the gold piles was a short young woman. Bundled up in a pink outfit with semi-transparent sparkling material over the legs, she certainly didn't seem like she had come prepared to go dungeon-delving. As she was spoken to, she opened her eyes, blue irises set against black sclera, and bounced with surprise. In an instant, she was up on her feet. As she moved, a single thick pink bang fell neatly over the middle of her face. It was a surprisingly long bang, considering the rest of her hair was short and framed her circular face. It was a face that showed surprise at being spoken to, expressive and bright, and just a little bit nervous.

"Oh, um, no. I mean, I'm having a hard time with my own connections. Not the electrical kind, but, you know--" Nuwa stammered, waving her gloved hands.

"Nevermind." Aster sighed and rose to her feet. "Louisa, please inform Lady Masamune that it will take another thirty minutes at least."

The final member of the group was also the tallest. With a slender teal and purple dress that hugged an angular body, she seemed as though she were about to walk a runway. Black hair with a slight wave framed her pale features and mint eyes. Her large dark ears twitched as she was called. Louisa strolled forward from the very back of the room. There, she had been observing something on her Chroniker. Her call to arms only served to put an annoyed frown on her features.

"Are you absolutely sure? I don't want to look like a fool if this isn't up to par when the time comes." Her voice was sharp and commanding, echoing faintly throughout the room.

"You're about to claim you went through a dark scary dungeon in that dress, Louie. I think you're gonna seem like a fool to someone."

"Clementine, was I speaking to you? No, I don't think I was. If your mouth runs like this during the broadcast, then you'll have to deal with myself AND Lady Masamune."

The bat-wielding woman tucked her weapon under one arm and held her hands up in mock surrender. Still, there remained a wide grin of amusement on her features.

"C'mon, Louie. I'll be on my best behavior, just for you. I'll be posing all obedient and cute, and all those wealthy assholes will be busting out bills like it's a strip-"

"Your analogy is unnecessary. Please avoid such subjects when we are in the presence of a child," Aster said quickly as she rose to her feet. She flashed Clementine an expression that was obviously an attempt at disappointment, but only seemed to flatten an already plain face.

"Child? What child? You talking about cotton-candy?" Clementine snorted, and turned towards the pink-haired girl.

She certainly seemed younger than the other three, but was still at least in her early twenties. As she was referenced, Nuwa snapped to attention once more. She had been focusing rather intently on the treasure chest in the center of the room. It was a spot that the broadcaster was now focused on and the eye circled around it in a wide fashion.

"Oh, me? It's okay, really. I know what strippers are. I don't think there's anything wrong with people taking off their clothes. I like mine on, but some people are more comfortable nude. I mean, I don't really understand it. Are taking clothes off symbolic of something? Maybe people are paying them because they have worked a hard day and they should be rewarded. When I work a long hard day, taking off my clothes always feels like a big show, so maybe that's it? But I think it would be much more impressive if they started peeling their skins off-"

"Okay, okay, okay. I'm not the one who needs their mouth watched." Clementine gave a hearty laugh, shaking her head. "Gods, where did Lady Masamune find this one?"

"It's not for us to judge Lady Masamune's choice of recruits. After all, Lady Masamune did recruit you." Louisa groaned. "You're sure that it's inside this chest?"

"The information we gathered said the compass had been dropped down into the abyss during the Wanderer's battle. The notes from Yamamoto stated that a dungeon on this asteroid held an incredible prize. Therefore, the natural conclusion is the nature of the chest's contents. But if you would like to open it before we film to check—"

"No. If the chest cannot be resealed then the viewers will question the validity of the chest. We cannot-"

"Yeah, yeah. Big moment, save it for the fans." Clementine groaned. "I came here expecting a good fight and an actual dungeon, and all of this has been a PR event."

Louisa gave a low and drawn out sigh. "Fine."

She opened a messaging app on her watch and sent a quick text.

Lady Masamune, we will be starting soon. I will make you proud.

THE perfectly carved tunnel leading away from the goo room was scarred by the Stardust deposits the group had seen earlier. It provided a faint glow as it shimmered and bounced off the new Insta-Light that Roanoke had lit a short time ago.

It was eerily silent; the mismatched group all lost in their own thoughts following the messy battle. Kaleida glanced at the faces both familiar and new, trying to get a sense of each person's status. It was difficult to gauge with most of them. Sungmin's face showed no difference from before the fight, and Maymay and Aki were too new. Aki seemed cheerful enough and their energy was almost infectious, but Maymay's haughty indifference tempered them. As for Roanoke... Kaleida chewed her bottom lip thoughtfully.

In the beautiful dim shimmer of the tunnel, Roanoke's features were both hard and pained. She knew without asking that he was feeling guilty and that she had probably hurt him. She wasn't ready to apologize to him, however. He had been an asshole; it was a part of him that needed to be called out. Still, she couldn't help but feel a similar sense of guilt. She didn't *like* being the bad guy. She wanted to be the cool guy. It wasn't fair. Silently, Kaleida's rainbow eyes darted up to Myth's thoughtful half-smile. As their eyes connected, she gave a slight nod in Roanoke's direction. Myth shrugged in response, and Kaleida's eyes narrowed in annoyance. More urgently, she nodded her head at Roanoke.

Talk to him, he mouthed.

Once more, Myth shrugged and frowned at her.

"Talk. To. Him," she whispered, voice tinged with annoyance.

"What do you want me to say?" Myth said with no attempt at being quiet.

Kaleida winced, and quickly looked back at Roanoke. There was no response or sign of acknowledgment from the man, and Kaleida exhaled deeply as she realized she had been holding her breath.

"Say something, you know, supportive? C'mon Myth, you gotta rally the troops! Or troop. Can one person be a troop?" Kaleida mumbled, nervousness making her ramble a little.

"Sorry you were a jerk, but hey you could have been worse?" Myth mused.

"You're terrible! How the Tartarus did you expect to lead a squad in the Academy?" Kaleida hissed back at him.

Myth rolled his eyes, but moved past her to walk next to Roanoke.

"HEY, buddy." his voice was so corny and forcefully peppy that there was no doubt he was trying too hard.

Roanoke stared straight ahead. His frown had only deepened. With Myth's not-so-quiet speaking and Kaleida having been right behind him, it hadn't exactly been hard to overhear their entire conversation. It only served to make him feel worse, and anger fought with appreciation over Kaleida's concern.

"What?" Roanoke distracted himself by pulling out his watch and looking over his stats.

"I was thinkin' after this we could swing by a Solar Burger. They got that limited edition double-nova spicy burger with canter sauce back in. I know you've been missin' those—"

"We'll see," Roanoke forced himself to say noncommittally.

The truth was, the mere mention of the burger caused his stomach to betray him with a loud groan. He knew what was happening, though. It was a common tactic used by adults to convince children not to pout. He wasn't about to fall for it. Besides, there was more on his mind than just the spat. His thoughts were going over all the little clues that he had picked up on during their little adventure. Those goo plushies at the gift shop, all of the literal signs, that room that seemed pretty obviously a cafeteria... What had they really stumbled into?

"HEY look, it's a checkpoint."

Kaleida's words were nearly lost on Roanoke. It was only when he collided with his sister that he snapped back to focus and looked around.

It was a strange small room. Beaten up dusty couches framed the smooth walls of the room. There were a few rectangular boxes that stood a little taller than a person spread around, but they were so worn with time that it was impossible to guess their meaning. Some were still standing, but most had been knocked over and collapsed. There were frames that likely once held pictures on the walls, and Roanoke's brow furrowed as he took the sight in. *What kind of dungeon uses artwork?*

"A checkpoint?" The peacock man strolled past them all and threw himself onto one of the longer couches. "What's that supposed to mean?"

"It's like what we had back at the academy. During the longer training dungeons, they'd put in rooms for the trainees to take a break and relax for a bit in. You could also sign your name on a sheet to prove that you got that far. This looks a lot like those rooms, only... more pathetic."

She gave a shrug and walked over to sit on another couch. The rest of the group began to disperse as well, with Sungmin grabbing one unoccupied couch and laying down on it. His eyes fluttered closed and, as everyone watched, his breathing became even and he fell into a light slumber.

"That man has no energy," Myth mused. The rest of the group nodded in solemn unison.

"Speaking of energy... you're already low on your levels, right? You and Paper Cut and the grumpy boy over there." Maymay gave a nod towards Roanoke, who pouted in response.

Kaleida quickly leaned forward. "Y-yeah, but it's not that big a deal. We have a couple Stardust boosters if we really need it. Normally I'd use a spot like this to rest for a while and let the levels naturally recharge... but even though there's a lot of Stardust veins in this place, there's not a lot of Stardust in the air to recharge me."

"And I'm runnin' outta cards," Myth pouted, slumping back.

"And yet you still expect to be able to get a Teien artifact. What's the point, anyways? What are a bunch of kids like you going to do with it?"

"Are you trying to find a CoS?" Aki's green eyes glistened with interest as they looked at the others.

"Yup! We need to." Kaleida perked up, but a look from Roanoke caused a strange pain to flash briefly in her eyes. "...It's important."

The room fell silent once more as the strained statement was left to linger in the air. Roanoke waited, mildly terrified that the pair would push for an answer of why it would be considered important.

He struggled to figure out something to say that could redirect the conversation.

"Which one are you looking for?" Aki's voice, much closer than it had been before, caught Roanoke completely off guard.

He turned to see the shorter figure only inches away from him. His rainbow eyes darted from the couch Aki had been on just a second ago and back to them with utter confusion.

Oblivious, Aki merely gave him an encouraging nod. "Are you trying to find someone special? Are you trying to find *the one*?"

"I'm not looking for a soulmate," Roanoke snapped, then immediately cleared his throat. "I mean... we're not looking for one in particular."

"I'd like to see you go up against Ankaa. She'd kick your ass." Maymay laughed from his couch, laying down on it like Sungmin had. "Oooh, or maybe Hokulei."

"Maybe Beijixing!" Aki suggested, causing the room to collectively shiver.

"I... don't think we're ready for the Final Frost. Ain't he the strongest one?" Myth stammered.

"Well, him or Vail." Aki shrugged. They leaned back a little. "They're both pretty scary, I think."

"I was thinkin' it'd be interesting to meet Delta." Myth smiled. "Heard she's one of the few good ones."

"We don't need a good one, Myth. Besides, it's debatable if any of them actually are." Roanoke nudged him and frowned softly. "You've got to keep focused."

"Delta's one of the nicest people you'll ever meet." Maymay rolled so he could look up at the ceiling, expression thoughtful. "Don't lump everyone together."

"You sound like you've had personal experience with her." Kaleida got to her feet.

"Do I? Perhaps I'm just more educated than you." Maymay flashed Roanoke a smirk and rose to his feet. Roanoke could practically feel his hair standing on end as every fiber of his being resisted the urge to fight him.

"Or maybe you're full of shit." Roanoke rose to his feet. "You think you know more than a ton of records throughout history?"

"You don't have to read a million books to know that some of those books are going to be wrong. Were you there when the Children of Stardust were created? Were you there when they supposedly killed the gods? Were you there when they got sealed? And were you there two years ago when—"

"Anyways, what Maymay's trying to say is that maybe they're not all super evil. I think the CoS are just like people. You're always going to have some bad ones, but maybe also those bad ones have changed." Aki smiled at Roanoke and gave him a nudge. "There's a lot of CoS that the records don't even talk about, you know. Maybe you've just got to meet them first."

"Break time's over. We should keep moving."

The physical contact was more than enough to push Roanoke away, but Aki's words lingered with him. While the various members of the group got up with varying levels of complaints, he recalled the earlier suspicion regarding Aki and their similarity to a CoS, but he also knew that pushing on it at that moment wasn't the best idea. If the pair really were CoS, as it seemed more and more like they might be, then to fight them now would be a near impossible battle. Even if they had managed to capture them, the issue of getting out of the abyss would keep them in the same position they were in before they had met the two. Once they got out, however...

"THIS is weird."

With her arms crossed over her chest and her cheeks puffed with annoyance, Kaleida surveyed the giant flickering sign that dangled by one chain from the ceiling. It said ***THE BOSS ROOM*** in large letters that likely once lit up, and was a less-than-intimidating greeting into the large and very dark room.

"Oh yeah, because the foam doors weren't." Maymay put one hand on his hip, holding back a snort.

"The dungeon's been awful helpful at pointin' things out for us." Myth chuckled, but he was as wary as the others.

"Where's the boss though?" Aki asked innocently as they looked around. The question caused the other three to tense.

"Roan!!!" Kaleida called out once more.

"What?" On command, Roanoke arrived at his sister's side. His rainbow gaze quickly took in the sign and he furrowed his brow.

"Insta-Light. Walk around the room, please." Kaleida waved one hand about the room as she delivered her order.

Roanoke gave his sister an exasperated look but pulled out a third Insta-Light. As it flew back up to circle around his head, he made his way to one edge of the room. The smell that had first come through the entryway was getting stronger. He could see Maymay pinch his nose and Myth wave his hat in front of his face. Even Kaleida brought her hat down over her face and nose. Sungmin pulled out a cloth mask and put it on without ceremony, leaving Roanoke as one of two without a cover. Only Aki seemed safe from the horrible scent as they stood and watched Roanoke do his walk.

Without any sort of hat or mask for himself, he brought his shirt up over his nose in a futile effort to combat the smell.

The room was wide enough that walking it actually took a bit of time. It was surprisingly barren, and the only interruption came with the presence of a door on the back wall. Unlike the first door, however, that one was actually metal and featured a true Stardust-enhanced lock. A quick exploration made it clear that the door could only be unlocked if a certain condition was met. A sign on the door read ***TREASURE ROOM.*** The group did not comment on it; they all knew what the others were thinking concerning the increasing strangeness of the place.

When the walk-around was complete, Roanoke made his way to the center to see if there was anything there that his light could find. As he stepped into the center of the room, he heard his sister gasp and looked over at her quizzically.

"Roan, look at the floor!" She pointed excitedly.

Roanoke turned his gaze downward obediently. A small circle laid directly below his feet, painted on a long time ago and barely illuminated by the light. Another circle extended beyond that... as did a third. He began to process the appearance of the three circles, trying to recall any particular symbols from Stardust casting that fit it. There wasn't any sort of trap or area spell that he could recall.

"Looks like a target to me." Myth chuckled, only for his laughter to fade as everyone registered the truth—and implications— of his words.

"Maybe you should—" Kaleida started to call out.

The sound of something groaning to life above Roanoke practically shook the space. They all looked up in time to see a massive dark shape surging downwards at Roanoke's body. Roanoke tried to move back, but it was hurtling too fast. In a pointless attempt at defense, he brought his arms up over his face and closed his eyes.

Instead of the pain of being crushed, Roanoke felt something slam into his chest and tackle him to the ground. He opened his eyes and saw Maymay over him, shielding him as a mess of metallic pieces fell about them. As Roanoke stared, a particularly sharp piece of metal fell onto the peacock man's shoulder and carved a deep cut into the flesh.

"Fuck, fuck, fuck," Maymay spat as his body tensed in pain.

"Roan!? Maymay!?"

Roanoke heard his sister on the other side of the large pile of metal. The scent they had all experienced earlier had become almost overwhelming with the fall of the pieces, but Roanoke's concern was directed to the man above him.

"How did you—?" Roanoke whispered, and Maymay shook his head.

"Used my air to propel me. That's a second thanks you owe..." Maymay trailed off as he groaned in pain. As Roanoke sat up, the others arrived.

"Maymay, that looks bad," Aki whimpered, going to their friend's side as Maymay took a seat on the ground.

"Really? Because it feels fucking nice..." Once more, Maymay's snark faded into a hiss of pain.

Kaleida moved to Roanoke's side and helped him up before looking to the taller man. "That was incredible. You saved him." She smiled brightly.

"Here." Roanoke moved quickly as soon as he was up. A quick dive into his inventory brought back two of the HP Ups he had taken from the ship.

"What's that?" Maymay grunted, but he had already extended one hand to take it.

"It'll help you heal. Carbonized healing potions with added flavor and vitamins and sugar," Aki explained, taking the second HP Up to hold for him.

"How do you know that?" Maymay flashed Aki a look that was a mix of confusion and annoyance.

"How do you not know that?" Aki frowned back at him. They leaned over and popped the tab on the drink for Maymay. "Drink it up before you bleed out."

"Fine." Maymay chugged the drink and the group watched as his purple eyes widened. He tilted his head back to get every last drop of the liquid, then dropped the empty can to look at them all with excitement. "That was amazing," he whispered, and grabbed the second one. That was downed faster than the first and the peacock man glanced about as though half-hoping Roanoke had brought out a third.

Maymay's wound began to heal quite rapidly. That was the power of higher end healing items, and though Roanoke was glad that he had it on him, he also mourned the loss of two expensive purchases. In less than a minute, Maymay was back up on his feet.

"I don't have to thank you now," Roanoke spoke quickly and turned away. "That counts."

Maymay opened his mouth to speak but seemed to think better of it. His lips were pressed into a thin line as he merely gave a nod of thanks. Aki wrapped their arms around their friend and hugged them tight.

"We're lucky they were around, Maymay. You can't heal yourself and I don't know any healing creatures."

Maymay opened his mouth once more to protest. Instead, he merely pinched his nose with his fingers.

"Has anyone else noticed the smell?" he whined.

The elephant in the room or, rather, the scent in the room, was finally given affirmation as everyone gave a nod.

"Over here." Sungmin, who hadn't joined everyone else, motioned for them as he stood on one side of the pile.

"What's up?" Myth asked as he was the first to approach. Sungmin pointed down and, as the others quickly moved in, they found the source of the scent.

With Roanoke's light and the lack of movement, it was now clear to see that the mess of metal had once been a dragon construct, although a poorly designed one. The face, which looked out at them with dead eyes, was almost cartoonish, as though it was made by someone who had never actually seen a dragon.

"That ain't a dragon," Myth confirmed, though no one actually needed the confirmation. "My family raises wyverns back on the ranch, so I know."

"Yeah, good thing you have that knowledge, or we'd never figure it out for ourselves." Maymay couldn't hold back the snort this time, though he frowned at the sight of it. "What's this doing down here?"

"That's not what I'm concerned about," Sungmin murmured through his mask. He motioned to the dragon's mouth. Inside of it, a cracked spout of some kind could be made out. It was leaking a strange looking black liquid.

"That's where the scent's coming from." Kaleida's eyes widened with realization. "But what is it?"

"Some kind of oil. Likely one that becomes toxic over time. And that is highly flammable." Sungmin nodded his head at a small gadget next to the source of the liquid, where a black crusted metal gave the indication that many fires had burned there over time.

"We shouldn't stay here. If it's that bad, then we're all going to get sick the longer we're around." Roanoke bit his lip as he considered things. "Until we can figure out what to do about that other door, we should go back to the checkpoint—"

"Dumb toxic dragon," Aki huffed.

They delivered a kick, far less powerful than Roanoke's had been, to the dragon's nose. A metallic and horribly broken roar came from a damaged voice box deep within the metal beast. The entire group leaped back; Roanoke somehow found himself holding Maymay and he quickly dropped him at the realization.

"Con...tions...turers...Treasure...yond.."

Clipped words echoed throughout the room, the source of them unclear. The sound of a musical beeping drew their attention to the other doorway; the Stardust lock on it glowed brightly for a moment before fading completely. An unlocking sound caused the group to exchange looks.

"Did... did we defeat the boss?" Myth finally ventured, scratching the back of his head.

"I'll take the win." Kaleida shrugged, making her way to the door. "Now c'mon, we need to get out of the creepy poisonous room."

No one was about to make an argument to wait. As everyone made their way through the treasure door, Roanoke kept his eyes on Maymay's back, tracing over the area of his shoulder blade where the cut had been. It left a strange feeling in his gut, as though he still wanted to thank the man despite his earlier words. However, his desire not to give Maymay the pleasure of hearing it was stronger than that gut sensation, and Roanoke resigned himself to merely ponder on Maymay's seemingly selfless act as they continued on.

chapter ten

ASTER'S ESTIMATE REGARDING the time needed to ready the broadcast was completely accurate, as the others had long since come to expect. The thirty minutes of waiting passed slowly. Clementine had started to get fidgety after ten minutes and Nuwa kept having to be directed back towards the rest of them. For Louisa, it was like herding children.

"It's ready, Louisa," Aster finally proclaimed in her usual monotone voice.

She rose from the broadcaster, which was now glowing stronger with power. The eyeball on it darted about as it took in the sight of everything. Around the room, there was a feeling of charged energy as the technomancy drew upon the natural Stardust reserve for fuel and to provide stability to the small construct.

"Sweet. I was just about to bust out the snacks and have a me day." Clementine twirled her bat around in her hand and struck it into the ground, leaning on it lightly as she waited.

"Snacks? I thought lunch wasn't until later..." The pink-haired girl up at the possibility of food, but the collective disapproving gazes she got from the others soon caused her to retreat.

Brushing off her group's dysfunctional handling of an important situation, Louisa made her way to the center of the room. Perfectly manicured fingers reached out to brush against the treasure chest seated perfectly on the pile, the golden rings on her fingers flashing in the light. The treasure chest was small and rather plain looking. It was outdone by the sheer show-factor of the rest of the treasures in the room, but focused lighting from above shone down on it to stress its importance.

"You're sure the broadcaster is ready, Aster?" Louisa asked one more time, her voice a little fainter.

"Yes. The connection is holding, and I have confirmation that Lady Masamune and her investors are standing by. You may begin at any time."

With a heavy nod in Aster's direction, the golden-ringed woman took her place in front of the chest. The sound of the broadcaster whirring to life filled the room.

Louisa turned to face the eye, her exasperated expression now replaced with a winning smile and proud pose. Aster stood politely to one side, making sure to avoid any sort of appearance on camera. In a completely opposite fashion, Clementine gave a broad grin and tried to strike a pose with her bat, which was the exact opposite of what she had promised the team leader. She brought one foot up to attempt to rest on the pile of gold, but the coins quickly gave out under her slight weight and Clementine ungracefully fell face-first into the gold. Nuwa, awkward and still apparently pondering on strippers who could strip off their skin, merely gave a casual wave to the camera as she looked nowhere in particular. At least, Louisa reasoned to herself, *she* would be perfect for Lady Masamune.

"After years of tireless research, Lady Masamune has done what no one else in the universe has. We have journeyed on her behalf to this dungeon, fought perils, and made it to this chamber in order to find the greatest treasure of all-"

"Geeze, did'cha write all this beforehand?" Clementine muttered. Louisa's eyes flashed with indignant fury.

"THE GREATEST TREASURE OF ALL—"

"LISTEN," Sungmin said suddenly.

Having been a distance in front of the group, he had been aware of the conversation in the back, but new sounds caused his attention to divert.

"What? Did you hear something?" Aki's small body darted in between the trio and practically slammed into Sungmin's back.

Sungmin gave a nod. Everyone fell silent, though it seemed Maymay was holding a great deal of input back. As they listened, the faint sound of voices greeted them. It was difficult to make out what the voices were saying, but Maymay grinned regardless and strolled forward.

"Well, well, well. Perhaps we'll be having some intelligent encounters," Maymay sneered.

"Or more intelligent company," Roanoke replied dryly. The peacock's purple eyes flared with indignation, and he opened his fan with a satisfying dramatic noise.

Before Maymay could come up with a snappy retort, Sungmin held one hand up.

"Shh. Let's get a little closer before we alert the masses to our presence, okay?" he whispered, voice tinged with faint amusement.

"Sounds like a plan to me," Myth said with a grin, voice booming.

"Seriously, do you even know how to whisper?" Kaleida grumbled.

Still, the group fell silent as they continued on. While they had been relatively distanced from each other previously, the situation at hand now brought them all close together as they attempted to sneak their way forward. It wasn't a long journey. They saw the light at the end of the tunnel soon enough, but paused as they realized there was no way to hide in the straight passageway. Sungmin brought a hand up to signal a stop as he started to appraise the situation, but Maymay and Aki didn't bother to acknowledge the silent instruction.

As the pair plowed forward, Kaleida and Myth offered Sungmin apologetic looks before following them. In the end, the four were far too curious and certainly not the stealthy types. It left Sungmin standing next to Roanoke. Though Sungmin didn't bother to look at Roanoke, assuming the man would disapprove of any sort of interaction, Roanoke chanced a look in his direction. Obviously struggling, Roanoke started to open his mouth. There was no time for him to say whatever it was he might have, however, as Sungmin gave a sigh and followed the rest of the group. Roanoke stood there for a moment, watching his newfound team leave him behind as they entered into the light. A knot twisted in his gut, something like memory dancing at the corners of his mind. He pushed those sensations aside for the time being and rushed in after them.

"-the Wayfinder's Compass! Kept sealed away in this chest, we shall now unveil this to the universe, and prove to all who doubt her that—" Louisa's speech continued as the group entered the room.

For a moment, the party stopped as they took in both the piles of gold and gems and the four women who were gathered around one small chest in the center of it. All but Louisa saw the group enter. Nuwa and Clementine exchanged looks of confusion, and Aster merely adjusted the glasses on her nose.

"Hey, Louie?" Clementine finally ventured, moving to Louisa's side.

"To all who doubt her that—"

"Don't wanna break your flow, but—"

Louisa stamped her foot, her heel digging into the earth and leaving a small dent. "I swear on the Stardust Sea, Clementine, if you interrupt me one more time, I'll—"

"We got company, babe." The bat-wielding woman gave a quick shrug and motioned with her weapon towards the group of six haphazard adventurers standing before them.

"Aww, you can continue your speech. I was really getting into it," Aki laughed, emerald eyes sparkling with delight.

"How did you find the compass too!?" Louisa sputtered. She turned sharply to face them, and her rings glinted in the light as she did.

"Wait, so the compass is here? Oh my gods, I was just pitching wild—" Kaleida gasped, utter triumph and delight dancing across her features.

"Don't play dumb with me!"

"It's in that chest, right?" Kaleida took a step towards the object, but the four women approached and formed a wall between it and Kaleida.

Instinctively, Roanoke and Myth moved to Kaleida's side and gave the other group a warning look. The tension in the room had surged. Sungmin, however, looked towards Maymay.

"Look, I got an idea. We beat the shit outta each other and the last ones standing can take the pretty chest, how 'bout it?" Clementine smirked, but the sound of gold tumbling over and falling captured all of their attention.

"I've got a better idea. Maymay and I take this, and the rest of you can fight it out from there." On top of the gold pile, Aki cradled the wooden chest to their clothed chest with a mischievous grin.

"You could have snuck away with it," Maymay gave a dramatic sigh.

"That's not any fun—"

Aki's proclamation was sharply cut off as the spiked bat slammed against their soft stomach. They went tumbling over the edge of the pile with a sharp gasp of pain. As they fell, the chest flew into the air and Aster fumbled for a moment before catching it.

"I do not enjoy fighting," Aster said in her robotic and mousy tone.

"Too bad. I do!" Kaleida snapped.

She hardly had time to process Aki and Maymay's apparent betrayal. A good fight was a great distraction, and she opened her inventory app. As she saw the dwindling supply of items, she winced. She hesitated for a moment but drew out her last stack of papers and her rifle.

Several paper bullets shot from Kaleida's rifle at Aster's face. The plain woman yelped and ducked out of the way, but tripped on her skirt as she did and went tumbling. The chest left her hands and rolled along the floor as the pair squared off.

It landed near Roanoke, and he wasted no time scooping it up with one arm. He created a long and sturdy silver sword, which he pointed directly at Maymay. The man had started to approach him but stopped as the sword was pointed at him, snorting in annoyance.

"So you were going to betray us?" Roanoke growled, hugging the chest a little tighter to his body.

"It was up in the air. Like you're going to be." Maymay shrugged. A swing of his fan shot a gust of wind at Roanoke and sent him flying up.

"Enough! This is my moment!" Louisa shrieked in frustration.

From her rings many thin but sharp wires shot out and wrapped around the chest. As she began to pull the chest to her, Myth stepped forward.

There was no time to count cards. It didn't matter that his stock was already dangerously low. With a focused stare, the man tipped his hat just slightly over his head. His Stardust activated, and he watched as the five top cards in his deck manifested in front of him. He quickly plucked the Three of Spades. With a flick of his wrist, he sent it flying at the pile Louisa was near. It collided with a plink of card hitting coin, and a mere second passed before a loud explosion could be heard. The gold went everywhere and pelted Louisa, who was already off balance from the explosion itself. Instinctively, the woman let go of the chest as she was assaulted by coins, and it continued its aerial travel.

Just as Myth was about to catch the chest, Aki jumped on his back, their arms wrapping around his neck. "Can I have it? Pretty please?" Aki cooed, and the pair began struggling as Myth did his best to shake them off of him.

A short distance away, Aster had gotten to her feet as Kaleida took a moment to make more bullets.

"It seems I have no choice but to participate. Very well. Let me show you what years of dedication to science have yielded!" Aster shouted, and Kaleida jumped at the way such a loud and gravelly voice came from the quiet and unassuming form.

"Wha...?" Kaleida started to speak.

Aster took off her glasses and tucked them safely in a glass case. As soon as the glasses left her face, faint lines like a computer chip's surface began traveling from her eyes through the rest of her body. Small lights flashed from various parts of her as the circuitry became complete. There was a pulse of energy, and Aster began to grow exponentially, like a middle school math problem. Her form became huge and bulky, and she glared down at the other woman with barbarian-like intensity.

"How does that even work—?" Kaleida whispered in disbelief.

Before she could react, Aster's massive hand gripped her body tightly. A guttural scream escaped the woman's mouth as she threw Kaleida into a wall.

Soon, the three-way battle had erupted into chaos. Clementine's ability quickly shone through. As she grabbed various gems and objects throughout the room, her hand superheated and charged them with kinetic energy. By the time she had tossed them up in the air and swung her bat at them, they had become mini bombs that sent the group scattering.

Louisa, with her wires, grasped at and tripped up the combatants as each got the chest. Her fingers moved as though she was controlling puppets. The wires cut into any cloth or flesh it touched, leaving most victims with deep cuts on their bodies. Aster focused solely on Kaleida, but didn't have any problems with throwing the girl towards other members of her group.

For her part, Kaleida was barely avoiding the worst of the damage, but Roanoke could see her status screen on her watch. The way her health bar was plummeting fast made his heart drop just as quickly. Maymay and Aki, the chaotic traitors, seemed more intent on grabbing the chest and running rather than participating in a full fight, but with both sides going after them, they had little choice but to contribute.

Surprisingly, however, Aki did not shapeshift as the battle went on. Their tiny form knew just the way to wiggle through the bodies that were being thrown about. They leaped over Clementine as the woman swung her bat, limboed under Louisa's wires, and rolled away from Myth's card effects. They weren't concerned with attacking. Instead, their vibrant green eyes constantly scanned the battle, looking for the treasure that everyone was fighting tooth and nail for.

In the midst of the battlefield, two did not participate. The blue-eyed Nuwa watched from behind one pile of gold, occasionally wincing as a flying body or exploding gem came a little too close to her. Her expression was twisted into a concerned pout.

"Do I? Oh, but what if I do? What if I don't? What if they get mad at me for ruining their fight? He wouldn't be very photogenic, I think. But Lady Masamune said..." The young woman mumbled to herself, her voice going a mile a minute as she seemed to put every single thought that she had into existence.

In a completely opposite manner, Sungmin stood still and silent close to the battlefield. His eyes were closed as he focused. It was unclear what exactly he was doing, but neon blood began to trickle down his cheeks like tears.

At that moment, Maymay grabbed the chest as it was flying through the air but found himself still the object of Roanoke's attention once more as he did so. The young man lunged at Maymay with his sword raised and face full of anger.

"You don't want to do this," Maymay growled at Roanoke, only for Roanoke to take an offensive stance.

"I really do." Roanoke launched himself at Maymay.

With every flick of his wrist, his sword lashed out at the peacock man, but he dodged all the blows. Maymay's own style seemed to be surprisingly disciplined. His body moved with a mix of dancer's grace and purposeful skill. Though he threw no punches, the wind became his weapon and Roanoke could feel the enchanted breezes slamming into him. He was being outclassed again, and he felt fury rising in his gut at his own weakness.

Roanoke's mind couldn't help but travel back to the battle against the knights, when he found himself caught. Back then, it was his artifact that bailed him out. No, more than that, it was....

He looked at Sungmin and gritted his teeth. He could play music for himself. He knew a few songs and their effects. He could...

His hand froze as it hovered over his Chroniker. A cold sweat broke out over his features as the young man hesitated. Memories so deeply carved into him that they didn't have to appear in his mind to keep hold of his body.

If I made another mistake like before... If I go out of control...

Fear paralyzed Roanoke until he felt a blast of wind slap him in the face. His hand left the Chroniker and he felt nothing but shame as he went back to simply using his weapon. The risk was too great, and he was still too weak. It took all of his skill just to finally land one good cut on Maymay's shoulder.

"Back off!" Maymay dropped the chest and put one foot firmly on it.

His purple eyes glowed golden as he stretched out a hand. His fan shifted and changed in his hands. It became more radiant, the plumage more striking, and the level of power that came off of it whipped around the room like a windstorm. Feathers fell around his body and the newfound power that burst from it was enough to turn all heads. As Roanoke saw the fan in its full glory and felt the power, he knew he had been right all along. Maymay was—

"A CoS!?" Louisa screamed, her voice strained.

"Golden fan... That's Mayura, right? Ain't he one the weakest one?" Clementine shrugged, not overly bothered by the development. In fact, her lips curled in an eager smirk and she grabbed a handful of gems.

"Excuse you!? I am NOT weak!" Mayura snapped, voice filling the space of the treasure room with a dramatic insulted tone.

"You all dared to bring a Child of Stardust into this!?" Louisa whipped around to face Roanoke with an accusatory expression, as though she was offended that they could have done something so horrible.

"We didn't know," Roanoke spat in return, but frowned again. "... Maybe we did. Kind of."

"I didn't," Myth called out from his side of the room, only to duck a moment later as another hail of high-charged gems came flying at him.

"This changes nothing." Louisa took a deep breath and raised her hands, the thin but sharp wires beginning to dance around the room once more. "We're taking that compass!"

"No you're--" Kaleida began to yell back, but Aster's giant fist slammed into her stomach.

Meeting strength that, at least temporarily, matched hers, Kaleida was flung back into one of the walls. The sound of her body slamming into it and the wall itself breaking at the impact was horrible. Roanoke watched with wide eyes as his sister fell, crumpled and unmoving, to the ground.

"Kal..." As he stared, he was overwhelmed with the sounds around him. The sound of the fighting, the sound of the gems and gold falling with every attack. The sound of his own breath and heartbeat. They were all too loud, but the one sound he wanted more than anything to hear was unheard. There was no response to his call. No sound of her moving to get back up.

He felt his body moving, but the individual actions were unclear. It was as though he had been possessed. His fingers brushed over his Chroniker, and he once again began cycling through his song list. Kaleida had gotten hurt. She had fallen while he had been holding back. Roanoke's walk turned into a run as he raced at the technological giant. He heard the first few notes of the song play before everything fell to utter silence.

It wasn't the first time he had lost sound. It had predated the nightmares. It was a dangerous obstacle to contend with when he already had enough trouble with his fetter and its ability. And he had already experienced what could come from it. But there was nothing that could hold him back now. Even without sound, he could feel his body surging with power, a power he wasn't familiar with and couldn't identify. The song must have been one he hadn't played before in this kind of situation. He didn't care; he had to help his sister.

With an unheard cry of anger, Roanoke lunged. His sword had changed into a scythe, which he wielded with ease. As he swung it down, the blade shimmered with silver energy that reflected various scenes, but he hardly paid attention. He saw Aster take a few steps back; she shouted something, but it was lost on him. What wasn't lost, however, was the quick movement that came from the corner of his eye. The unassuming pink-haired girl who had mostly watched the battle from afar stood protectively in front of Aster. She held a long and somewhat strange looking pink and yellow axe that looked more like a gaudy toy than anything. Roanoke's scythe collided against her axe as she held it firm. He was surprised by her strength and speed, but it wasn't going to stop him. His eyes burned with determination as he used all of his strength to press down on her weapon.

The blade shimmered powerfully as it made contact with her axe. Roanoke watched as the silver that had glowed around it seemed to travel to her weapon as well. The pair stared wide-eyed as a circle formed at the point where their blades connected. It was soon recognizable as a portal, for Roanoke could see the interior of the circle showing the peak outside of the abyss.

The pink-haired girl opened her mouth and said something. Her expression was that of innocent and genuine confusion. His own expression betrayed the same. But before either could pull their blades away, the portal exploded between them. Roanoke felt himself being dragged into it with so much force that he could not find any resistance in his weary battle-beaten body. He looked out the portal as he fell through to see everyone in the treasure room looking at them with fear and surprise. Sungmin ran towards the portal, but Roanoke's gaze moved instead to look upon his sister's unconscious form.

I'm sorry, Kal.

chapter eleven

ROANOKE AWOKE TO THE FEELING of cool stone against his cheek. His body ached as he pushed himself up enough to look down, and his world spun as he found himself looking at the abyss. The young man scrambled backwards before he realized that he was laying on the peak that he and his teammates had stood on in what felt like forever ago. He was back. He had made it out. His heart pounded in an instinctive burst of joy, but it was quickly crushed as he realized the reality of the situation. The others were still down there.

He gave a silent scream and slammed his fist into the rock. He had been reckless again. A teleportation ability? He raised his hand to try and activate the power once more, but found no weapon there. Instead, it laid in pieces just off to the side of him. It took only a quick glance at his Chroniker to confirm that his Stardust levels had depleted so low that he couldn't sustain a weapon with the fetter's ability empowering it.

He gave a hollow laugh and dug his fist against the stone, feeling the bits of gravel embedding themselves into his skin. Was the universe really fucking with him at that moment? Did it really want to have a laugh at his expense? Despair flooded him; he thought about leaping off the peak and back into the abyss. Either he would die, or he'd find some way to land and then he could go back. Both felt desirable at that point.

A faint song echoed in his ears; the first sound he had heard since his hearing had disappeared in the battle. It was the familiar one, the one that he had heard several times since arriving at the rest stop. And it came from the place his fist had punched. Fear and curiosity mixed and, slowly, he raised his red-knuckled hand to look down. His inhuman strength had broken some of the stone away to reveal small Stardust veins running through the peak. It sounded like the song was coming from them.

It was a strange thought, and one that he was certain came as a sign that he had totally lost it. Unable to help himself, drinking in the familiar song like it could be a healing soda, he slowly leaned down and put his ear to the veins. He strained to hear the song, to get a clearer sense of it. To understand why it felt so familiar...

"It's a gorgeous view, ain't it? You always did know how to pick them."

Roanoke jolted up at the sound. The voice who spoke was unfamiliar to him and he hadn't heard anyone approach. His eyes opened to see two boots standing just in front of him. His gaze trailed upwards. A figure in a white cloak adorned with the Wanderer's symbol on the back stood in front of him on the very edge of the peak. Beyond it, where once was the deep darkness of the abyss, a river of colors and light weaved past them and off into the distance. The one who stood before this river was short and thin. Though there was nothing else that could be observed about their appearance, some part of Roanoke knew who it was. The picture on the postcard seemed to come alive in front of him.

"You've gotta put a stop to this, Saros. I know you're capable of bein' a good person. I want to help ya change. But I can't do that until you give us the compass. Let us take the Children of Stardust and use them to make somethin' new outta what they destroyed."

Roanoke turned in the direction of the voice. Beyond them was a crowd of figures. They were shadowy and most unidentifiable, though various sizes, races, and forms could be made out. There was an overwhelming sense of anger and power that came from the crowd. Roanoke couldn't help but tremble a little bit at it.

Standing in front of it at all was a tall man with a broad chest. He looked to be older, with a roughly shaved chin and features that could be called handsome. Stormy grey eyes peeked out from sun-tanned skin, and dull blonde hair pulled into braids fell about his shoulders. His attire was rough and casual with an open-chest white shirt and trousers. At his side were several different swords.

Roanoke knew immediately who the figure was. All of the records talked about him: The Pirate King James, the God of Storms who ultimately took down the Wanderer and brought him to an eternal prison.

The pirate king didn't seem to register Roanoke's existence. He took a few steps towards the other figure. The grin on his features was warm and reassuring, and his voice had been kind and pleading, but at the close distance, Roanoke could see a darkness in those eyes. It was like peering into the clouds of an approaching storm. When the

Wanderer didn't respond, James sighed and put a hand on one of his weapons. The blade was long and the blade jagged, with pieces of cloth still hanging from its edges.

"I know. You want to protect what you've created. I get it. I really do. But face the truth, Saros. The sword that killed and absorbed your fellow gods. The sword that destroyed your star. The Children of Stardust! Your creations are dangerous and need to be controlled!"

The figure tilted their head slightly towards James. Roanoke felt his whole body go numb, though he could hardly guess why.

"And you're going to be the one to control them?"

The Wanderer's voice. There were incredibly few still existing in the universe who had ever heard it. A gentle and quiet tone with an almost musical-like quality to it. James frowned at him.

"I'm your friend. They all want justice. Just give us the compass and we'll go out and find them. Ya don't have to keep runnin'."

The Wanderer was silent for a moment. Murmurs were beginning to build among the massive crowd behind James. They were unintelligible words, but the hatred and raw pain was clear. James' fingers curled ever so slightly around the hilt of the sword.

"I sealed them away."

The Wanderer turned to face the crowd. Though Roanoke's heart had frozen with anticipation at seeing the god's face, what greeted him was a black mask with neon accents. It was styled as a fusion between a peacock and a butterfly, and the prismatic eyes of a Teien burned through them as he looked at the group.

"What!?" James' smile dropped as his voice growled with a primal rage. *"How did you—?"*

"Did you think I'd just let you all find me like this? You know me better than that. I had to make sure you were all distracted so I could safely put each in their stasis. The time it took for you all to

gather up and arrive was more than enough. Thank you, James. I can always count on your pageantry."

"*This... this ain't pageantry.*" James' voice shook with anger and his mouth twitched as he tried and failed to return his grin. "*These are all people who want justice for what those weapons did! And I want peace for you!*"

"*I know what you want, James. I've given you enough of it already.*" The Wanderer turned his gaze from James and to the crowded mass. "*They won't cause you trouble again... at least, not for a long time. Once someone who truly needs them wakes one up, they all will follow. And if they bring new chaos, then... I will watch that universe fall to it. Chaos is change. The Children of Stardust are—*"

An angry roar cut the Wanderer off. James lunged at him, his vicious sword pulled out and slashing with a powerful Stardust aura at the other god. The Wanderer stumbled back and, as they did, they fell backwards against the peak. Roanoke watched as they fell half into the river. Though James was gearing up for a second attack on the seemingly helpless Wanderer, Roanoke's attention was wholeheartedly on the infamous being. It was difficult to see at first, but as Roanoke squinted, he noticed it. From the right sleeve of the Wanderer's cloak, a compass slipped purposefully into his hand. Roanoke watched as the gloved hand clutched tightly to the compass for only a moment before he let go.

The small object, glowing from a prismatic core in the center of it, sunk deep into the water. Its shine and, indeed, the very appearance of it, was difficult for Roanoke to make out against the colorfully glowing river even at his close distance. It disappeared within seconds. Roanoke turned to look back just as James' sword plunged down at his and the Wanderer's body.

"*The Children of Stardust are ours!*"

In an instant, it was all over. Roanoke gasped; his chest was begging for air. It felt like he had been drowning. He was also keenly aware that he was being shaken quite roughly by the shoulders. His hazy gaze focused from the vision that he had been submerged in. The first thing he could see was the color pink, and a lot of it. His eyes sharpened slowly but surely and he was able to see that the mass of pink shaking him was none other than the girl who had been with the enemy team back in the treasure room. Her bright blue eyes, set against black sclera, peered at his face at an unnecessary close distance. She was speaking, but Roanoke was both confused and frustrated to find that he still heard no sound.

With an angry huff, he shoved her away and jumped up. As soon as he did so, he regretted the action. His body fell back like a doll who had been picked up and expected to stand on its own. Before he could hit the floor once more, the girl grabbed his shirt once more.

As soon as she let go, his weak body began to collapse once more. Again, the girl grabbed him, and Roanoke was annoyed to find there was a hint of innocent amusement in her gaze. She loosened his grip and he started to fall again. He scowled at her, but she seemed more interested in the predicament. She let go of him again and reached out her hand but, this time, Roanoke wasn't about to play her game. He slapped her hand away and promptly fell backwards, slamming his head against the stone and moaning at the pain.

The girl laughed. At least, Roanoke thought she did. She had covered her mouth, but he could see her shoulders jumping up and down.   He wanted nothing more than to fight her; she was a member of the group that had hurt his sister. She hadn't taken advantage of the situation to hurt him, however. At least, not unless she sincerely thought that shaking him could cause actual damage. But if that was the case, Roanoke reasoned, she still had her long axe laying just a bit off to the side.

His head was so filled with the vision he had just experienced and the fight before it that he couldn't really figure out what to do. He was still angry at himself and he was certainly still terrified for his sister. Myth and Sungmin were also in danger, especially now that the Children of Stardust had turned on them. There was something about the conversation between James and the Wanderer that nagged at him, but it was hardly the time to analyze the scene.

He pulled himself to sit cross-legged on the ground and stared at the girl with exasperated expectation. At least if she attacked him, he could focus on that in the moment instead.

Instead, the girl began chatting at him. With how quickly her mouth was moving, it was impossible for Roanoke to even attempt to read her lips. He soon gave up; his head hung low against his chest as he realized whatever the girl wanted, it certainly wasn't a fight. His body was so tired he didn't think he could lift it up enough to walk away, either. He briefly entertained the idea of rolling himself off the edge of the cliff, but he knew deep down that he couldn't do it, despite his earlier thoughts.

Kaleida had been right about the compass. Sungmin had been helpful. He had spent the whole dungeon in stubborn defiance of both but, in the end, they had it together, and he didn't.

I could have asked Sungmin for a song back there.

Roanoke's eyes opened a little wider. He was surprised that the thought had popped into his head, but he couldn't disagree with it. And as for the two Children of Stardust... Roanoke thought back to the vision. It'd be easy to keep defining them as the weapons they were created to be. Yet, hearing the way James talked about them, Roanoke couldn't help but feel a twinge of disgust at the sentiment.

Sure, Mayura was the biggest dick he had ever met, but he wasn't just some weapon. An object wouldn't be owed the kind of ass-kicking Roanoke wanted to give him.

Satisfied by the thought, Roanoke's prismatic eyes flashed with determination. He looked at her and quickly looked to the side as he felt unease setting in. "... Do you know a way to get back there?" he asked, though he still couldn't hear his own voice.

Immediately, the girl began to speak rapidly.

He gave a deep sigh and ran a hand over his face. It wasn't her fault; he knew that. It was still incredibly frustrating though. Whatever she had been saying, however, became punctuated by movement. The girl hopped up and offered him an encouraging smile. Once more, Roanoke had to remind himself that this girl had been on the enemy team. Even though he hadn't seen her actually do anything beyond defending the person who had hurt his sister, she hadn't done anything to stop them either.

Roanoke watched as the girl put her hands over her heart. Around her, energy began to rise from the stone. The Stardust vein he sat near surged upwards in a beautiful light show. He could feel his body recharging with Stardust energy as it was pulled from the earth itself. He couldn't help but stare in awe. *Geomancy.* He had never seen it in action before, but he had certainly heard about it. To be able to gain power from the star itself on a level and in a way that far differed from other users... It was a rare skill indeed, and he certainly wouldn't have expected it from someone who didn't seem all there.

She picked up her long axe and beckoned him towards her. It took all of his effort, though the rising energy helped give him a bit more power. He hesitated as his hand reached out to take hers. Every part of him still felt apprehension at the thought of getting close to someone else in that way... In any way. But he couldn't let it hold him back. Sucking in his breath, he slowly placed his hand in hers. He felt the pressure of her hand squeezing his in what seemed to be a comforting manner, though he couldn't be entirely sure. The world around them began to spin and, as Roanoke looked from her hand to her face, the world faded completely to a whirlwind of color.

chapter twelve

THE GROUP RETREATED BACK to the checkpoint room, where the couches served as beds for the injured. On one side of the room, Myth laid out Kaleida and Sungmin's unconscious forms on the furniture pieces. The wyvernboy opted to stand, and he settled on digging through the inventory on his Chroniker.

There were a few minor healing sodas left, and a half-used Stardust booster, both of which he was hesitant to use on himself despite both his health and Stardust levels being dangerously low. His inventory was pitiful and dotted mostly by the random items that he had looted from the remains of the ooze. The two things that he was looking for, however, were the two things that he did not have.

His current deck had run down to the last five cards, and he hadn't been able to get a replacement deck yet. His Stardust energy had run so thin that, even if he did have a full deck on hand, the wyvernboy wasn't sure if he would be able to utilize it. And the last item, the most important, was the item that his group had the worst trouble getting ahold of: A revival tea, which could get Kaleida conscious faster.

Searching for the items provided a good distraction from the current situation. The unanswered question about where Roanoke went gnawed at the back of his mind and threatened to pull to the forefront if he didn't find something else to focus on.

On the opposite side of the wide room, Mayura leaned against the wall with his arms crossed over his chest. At his side, Aki fumbled with their hands nervously as they looked over the wounded party. Several times, the shorter figure opened their mouth as though to speak but could not muster anything to say. They looked helplessly to Mayura, but the man's gaze was focused on the three. There was a tense silence as both sides kept at bay. It was too much, and soon Mayura's face twitched with a strange sort of annoyance.

"What are you looking for?" he called out to Myth, his voice echoing in the empty room.

The wyvernboy shot him a look, not bothering to respond as he continued his search. He had poured over the same twenty-five boxes several times now, but he was trying to convince himself that, perhaps, he had merely overlooked the item that he had needed. Without a response, Mayura was only further motivated. He took several long strides forward. Immediately, Myth had moved between him and the others. His body shook with pain and exhaustion but a strong and defiant expression, rare for him, shone on his features.

"Back to your traitor side, CoS," Myth growled. His hand instinctively went to the deck kept at his side. The few cards left felt both heavy and empty between his fingers.

"Oh, is that what we're calling it now? You should have told me sooner, I would have drawn a line."

"Ya drew a line when ya started fightin' us back there," Myth growled, his accent growing heavier with his anger.

Before Mayura could continue the argument, a prismatic rainfall began to fall from the stony ceiling. It was a rather beautiful and delicate obtrusion to their tense moment. Both stared in puzzlement, and puzzlement became absolute disbelief when, from the rain, Roanoke's body fell to the floor.

"Roan!" In an instant, Myth had moved to Roan's side and helped the young man up. Roanoke gave him a single look. "Where'd you go!? I was worried sick— " Myth paused and took in the expression on Roanoke's face. "Your hearing...?" he muttered in a tone so quiet it escaped Mayura's nosy ears. The two had known each other long enough for Myth to pick up on some things.

The wyvernboy had asked the question so slowly that Roanoke was able to read his lips, and he merely nodded in response, then quickly looked around. As soon as his prismatic eyes found Kaleida's body on the couch, he raced to her side and took her hand. As soon as he was situated at her side, Roanoke seemed to take on a guard dog-like pose. His gaze moved to take in Sungmin's unconscious form and he frowned further.

"Ah..." Myth moved over to Roanoke. Outside of Mayura's view, he brought up his Chroniker and typed.

Things went from bad to worse when u left. They got Sungmin too and said they'd kill them both if we didn't leave. The peacock got them to let us take them both out, but now we can't get in there. It's all covered in those creepy wires.

ROANOKE scanned the words and felt his heart plummet. His sister looked so vulnerable and beaten lying there... and he could see neon blood trickling from perfect lines around Sungmin's wrists and neck. The fact that it was Mayura who had gotten them both out of there though... once more, doubt filled Roanoke's gut. He quickly pulled up one of his apps, the one that translated spoken words into text that he could follow, desperate to get more information.

In the meantime, Mayura had had enough of the secret conversation. "Welcome back. Glad you're not dead. Where'd you go, by the way?" the tall man asked in a half-bored monotone voice.

Roanoke glanced at the words but gave no answer; he was busy looking around the rest of the room. The pink girl who had previously traveled with him was nowhere in sight. Where had she gone? He chewed his bottom lip as he tried to come up with some answer.

His lack of response evidently annoyed the peacock man. Mayura rolled his eyes but knelt down in front of Kaleida. He brought one hand out but, as he did, Roanoke's hand shot out to grab his wrist. Mayura jolted in surprise and faced him. With a deep sigh, Mayura attempted to shake his arm loose from Roanoke's hold. He found, however, that the other's grip was surprisingly tight.

"You can let go. I'm going to heal her," Mayura muttered.

Roanoke didn't respond; though the words appeared for him, they gave no tonal indication of just how honest the peacock man was, but just the sight of the man's face was still fueling the growing anger in him. They had already messed with them enough.

"...Ya can wake her?" Myth frowned more.

"I can try." Mayura wrenched his arm away from Roanoke's and nearly fell back. With a frustrated huff, the purple-eyed man rose to his feet and looked around. He spotted what he was looking for; just beyond them there was a thick vein of crystallized Stardust embedded in the rock. "You have to let me give it a shot, though."

"Ya jokin'."

"Look, I don't have the time for this. The fact of the matter is, without any way to wake those two up, there's no chance of any of you getting out. You can't go and fight lady's night out back there, and there's nothing to be gained by us bringing your party up to full. See? Easy logic for you to grasp." Mayura groaned. He brought one hand to his gorgeous wavy hair, absently pulling it over his shoulder.

Myth was silent as he processed the words. The whole conversation had been transcribed on his app, and Roanoke studied them thoughtfully. They certainly had logic to them, as much as they pissed him off. They had no choice... his rainbow eyes scanned Sungmin, Kaleida, and Myth. Mayura was right. It was something he hated to admit, but he wasn't afraid to throw away his pride for the sake of his friends. As he caught Myth's gaze, he offered the man a nod before turning his attention back to the peacock man.

"All you're gonna do is heal 'em?" Myth stated slowly.

"And the two of you, if you'll let me," Mayura said, and directed his powerful gaze back to Roanoke. The two shared a tense stare as Mayura awaited a response. As the peacock man's impatience grew, Myth broke the silence.

"Uh, he can't hear ya," Myth said faintly, though Roanoke knew that wasn't the whole reason for his silence.

"Excuse me?" Mayura whirled around, his silk and scarves and golden accessories twirling with his lithe form.

"He, uh... he's got a condition. Sometimes his hearin' just... ya know, it stops? Can't predict it or nothin'," Myth tried to explain as briefly as he could.

Mayura sighed once more. Still, his purple eyes held a faint pain to them. "Well. I'm not sure about chronic conditions. But I will heal all of you the best I can."

Mayura knelt down in front of Roanoke once more. His body tensed and he rose a little out of instinct, and Mayura's mouth twitched as he held back an amused look. He studied Roanoke for a moment, then raised one of his fans in the air. As he did so, golden feathers created a curtain and, as the curtain pulled away, purple glittering letters had formed in the air.

I AM GOING TO HEAL YOU ALL. HATE ME IF YOU WISH. BUT I WANT YOU TO HATE ME WHEN YOU'RE BACK TO 100%.

Roanoke read the words in the air quickly. He tried to glare, but it lasted for seconds before his weariness sank in. Truthfully, he was in pain, and his body was tired. Just like Myth, he was at low levels on all fronts, though his Stardust levels had gone up thanks to the pink girl. Even his anger towards Mayura was starting to fade into tearful resignation. He wanted to disbelieve the peacock man just as much as he wanted to believe him. Roanoke finally gave a short and stiff nod, bringing one hand to hold Kaleida's.

WITH the approval, Mayura exhaled and stood up. He began to walk towards the vein that he had spotted earlier, and both of the men watched him with cautious curiosity.

"Maymay, you sure you're gonna be alright?" Aki asked.

No one had noticed it but, just as before, the shorter figure had seemingly moved with no movement. They stood beside Myth, and the man jumped back out of reflex at the sudden presence. Aki's green eyes surveyed their friend with concern.

"Alright is not a word to be applied to anything that's happening right now," Mayura said with a snort.

He stopped in front of the vein and took a deep breath. His fan disappeared from his possession, and he flexed his now-empty hands with quiet consideration. Slowly, he placed one hand on the vein. As soon as the contact occurred, Mayura's body surged with Stardust power. He gasped as he felt it hit him and fill him. It was the sensation of plunging deep into an ocean and feeling the saltwater fill the lungs. It was a sensation he had experienced only a few times before. For a CoS, it was like placing a bowl of gasoline near an open spark. Yet, Mayura knew what he needed right now was an eruption of inner flames.

He danced the edge of overdosing and yanked his hand back as the sensation of drowning began to make his head swim. The world had begun to fade into lights and colors and darkness, and all of it was far too welcoming for the peacock man's liking.

When he turned back to the others, he swayed like a drunken man. "Oooh..." he moaned quietly, and started to feel himself falling before Aki was there to hold him up.

"C'mon. Let's get you over there," Aki said softly and offered their companion a bright smile.

Mayura returned it as best he could, but his wavering expression suggested he was barely registering the reassurance. As soon as Aki brought him back to the side of the unconscious party members, Mayura fell to his knees. The air around them began to swirl as golden feathers, purple, teal, and blue sparkles of Stardust mixed into a whirlpool of wind. It was a beautiful sight, and he could tell that Roanoke and Myth couldn't help but appreciate the splendor of it.

As the feathers fell on them all, they seemed to melt into their skin. With each contact, Mayura could see the relief washing over them like a cool breeze. Before long, he knew their pain and exhaustion had mostly vanished. A quick glance at their status app told them that their bodies had been restored to full health and that they had gained a touch of their Stardust levels back.

With a triumphant smirk, Mayura slumped back in a daze.

AS soon as Roanoke saw this, he immediately turned his attention away from the dramatic display and towards his sister. He gave her hand a squeeze. He waited with baited breath for any sign of waking. Indeed, the wounds on her body had all but vanished.

Come on... He thought urgently, as though he could shove the thought into her head like a morning alarm.

Myth, too, had moved closer to her and Sungmin's sides. A look of weariness took over Mayura's features while they did. The peacock man's eyes fluttered half-closed as he watched them all.

"Roan?" Kal's voice, slightly dry, spoke up over the silence.

Her rainbow eyes opened and immediately met that of her brother's. Roanoke, who had not heard her voice, merely grinned weakly at her. Kaleida grinned back and sat up to pull her brother into a tight hug.

"What's with that dumb smile, you nerd? You know your sister can't be beaten that easily," she whispered, but her voice was shaky as she fought back tears.

Roanoke didn't have to hear Kaleida's words or look at his app to know what she was saying. He knew her well enough. Instead, he simply hugged her tighter.

"Nice to have ya back to the world of the livin', Kal. You're awful good at scarin' us," Myth sighed, but he wore a grin as well.

"It was just a nap." Kaleida shrugged in a non-committal fashion. She pulled Roanoke off her gently and began to look him over for injury. As she did, her eyes met his and she realized the situation just as quickly as her brother had known her words. "His hearing?"

"Faded out durin' the battle," Myth muttered.

"Damn." Kaleida scratched her head but noted his app still up. "Roan, you're okay, right?"

The words spelled out quickly on the projected screen, and Roanoke gave an urgent nod as soon as he saw them.

"Good," Kaleida sighed. Soon, however, she began to realize the full effect of the situation. "Wait a minute, what happened with the fight? How am I healed? What about the CoS—"

"Lost the fight. I healed you. We're right here," Mayura said in a somewhat sleepy fashion, giving a wave from his position resting against Aki.

"You!" Kaleida was quickly up on her feet.

"I know, I know. We're terrible beings who betrayed the trust you gave us five minutes after meeting us. But we had a good reason for it."

"And we didn't really want you to get hurt like that! I thought you could handle it..." Aki mumbled, their head hanging in shame. "I didn't realize you all were so low level—"

"That's not the point!" Kaleida snapped. "We were so close! Do you know how long we've been looking for that compass!?"

"To find a CoS, right?" Mayura said dryly, raising an eyebrow.

"Right! We have six months to get that compass and find a CoS before we're all officially out of the P-300!" Kaleida stamped one foot indignantly.

"P-300?" Mayura tilted his head in genuine questioning.

"Phoenix 300. It's a big organization in the universe now, Maymay. They have a lot of fancy powerful people who go all over the place to help people. Like bounty hunters with a brand name," Aki explained to Mayura quietly.

Mayura blinked and looked back at his friend. "How do you know that?"

"How do you not know that? We've been awake for two years now..."Aki groaned.

"Hello? I'm not done scolding the two of you," Kaleida said, and stamped her foot once again for extra effect.

"Why do you have to find a CoS just to get in with some Sea cops?" Mayura asked, glancing back at Kaleida and yawning. "Seems like a ridiculous entrance requirement."

The room fell silent once more. Kaleida's words had been quickly appearing on the holographic screen as she had been talking, and Roanoke had been taking every word in. Kaleida bit her lip.

"I messed up." She admitted after a painful amount of silence. "We were all trainees, and I screwed up real bad. My mom... uh, one of the heads of the P-300 said if we could catch one of the CoS, they'd let us back in. But we had a year to do it and it's already been six months. I'm the reason Roanoke and Myth's dreams were taken away from them, so... so it's my job to get it back. I took away the experience of them having an adventure, having a team, and—"

"Well, you found us," Mayura said sharply, his voice apparently cutting through her rambling.

Kaleida paused, his words having disconnected her from her guilt.

"Yeah. You found two CoS at once! I think that's pretty impressive." Aki grinned in support.

"That's... That's right," Kaleida said slowly, looking between the two of them. "You're—"

"Aquila, the Dynamic Roc. Shapeshifter Supreme. And Mayura the—"

"The Phantasmal Peacock. King of Air and Illusions," Mayura said, back on his feet and posing just in time for his introduction.

"And no one was surprised by that," Kaleida couldn't help but mutter dryly, a somewhat bitter smile spreading across her features.

"I mean, I kind of was," Myth said quietly, his voice bordering on a pout.

"I didn't realize the Phantasmal Peacock had healing in their repertoire." Sungmin's tired voice rang out, and everyone turned to look at him. He had sat up but was resting his chin back on his guitar case. The instrument holder had, surprisingly, no trace of damage from the fight and still provided a suitable head-rest.

"I... I taught myself," Mayura mumbled. A dark blush passed over his features. "Well, someone else taught me, but... I learned it after we were all awakened."

"I thought CoS could only use the Stardust types that the gods they were made from used?" Myth said, slowly sliding into a sitting position on one of the couches.

"Hence my needing a fuck ton of extra magic to be able to do that healing. Us CoS have unlimited energy for the magic we're created with. But anything we learn outside of that takes an annoying and separate amount of magic—er—Stardust," Mayura explained, but it was obvious from his tone that his patience for explaining things was wearing thin.

"And why would two CoS be on the hunt for a compass that can find any of you?" Sungmin asked, his voice so soft it was nearly lost in the conversation. The newly identified Aquila pouted.

"That's... Well, Maymay and I are trying to stop Kani!"

"The Spider's Cut? Isn't she one of you?"

"Don't lump us all together. The CoS aren't all evil, you know," Mayura grumbled, and summoned one of his fans to resume fanning himself.

"Right, you just killed a bunch of gods and caused a bunch of chaos three hundred years ago—" Myth began to speak, but a sharp elbow to the gut from Kaleida silenced him. Mayura and Aquila tensed at his words.

"... That aside, the CoS aren't exactly all buddies. I go after kings and queens, not peasants. I'm not interested in ruling anyone." Mayura hid his mouth with his fan, but his purple eyes had grown hard. "Kani's decided she wants to become a queen. She's been going by the name Lady Masamune and—"

"And she's been doing a lot of scary things in the Seieungha Sphere. She's been attacking smaller stars and bringing them under her control by killing or bribing their lords. Those people were probably some of her followers," Aquila said quickly, their high-pitched voice practically tripping over the words.

"And she's seeking the compass as well. We thought we might be able to grab it before she did. I'm not sure why she wants it, but I do know something she wants is something I'd be happy to take from her." Mayura snapped his fan closed. "We're here to disrupt the plans of a dangerous CoS. That's all."

Sungmin was quiet and thoughtful for a moment as he took in the long explanation. Finally, with a yawn, he rose to his feet and put his guitar case on his back. "The three of you need to catch a dangerous CoS, right? That's the whole purpose of finding the compass?" He asked, turning slightly to Myth, Kaleida, and Roanoke.

"W-Well, yeah..." Kaleida relented, her anger having been replaced with subtle confusion as she tried to sort out her feelings.

"Then it seems your goals are one in the same. For better or worse, it serves everyone's purpose to work together against those women in there. We don't have to like each other, we just have to not like them," Sungmin said simply.

His words appeared on the screen for Roanoke in bright glowing letters. Roanoke pursed his lips, then slowly nodded in agreement. Sungmin noted the response and knelt in front of the man, who had yet to leave the floor for one of the couches.

"Sungmin, Roan can't—" Myth started to interject.

"I know," Sungmin responded simply.

As his pale red eyes stared into Roanoke's rainbow gaze, he leaned in slowly. Roanoke, flustered at the closeness, quickly inched back until he hit the wall. His face flushed a dark red, but Roanoke could hear a new voice inside his head.

We're going to work together. We're going to defeat them. Can you trust me to help you do that?

Roanoke recoiled in utter surprise and, in the process, slammed his head against Sungmin's. The latter fell back, but the corners of his mouth pulled slightly in a small smile. Roanoke stared at the man in utter disbelief. As Sungmin got back up, his voice spoke gently in Roanoke's head once more.

I can sync with all of you. That means I can talk to you like this. I'm sorry if that surprised you.

Roanoke narrowed his gaze at Sungmin, despite his remaining blush. He simply looked away in a huff and crossed his arms over his chest.

"Not sure what's goin' on there, but even if we work together, ya think we really stand a chance against them? Kal and I are just about outta supplies and still low on Stardust. Roan's deaf, and those two—" Myth jutted one thumb at the pair of CoS "—still ain't trustworthy."

"You don't need a lot of supplies or Stardust to defeat an enemy," Sungmin said quietly. He turned his pale eyes on each member of the group, who stared at him expectantly. He made a sound that seemed to be a mix of a yawn and a sigh.

"Well? Care to elaborate?" Mayura said after a moment, tapping his closed fan against his arm impatiently.

"You don't need a lot of supplies or Stardust to defeat an enemy," Sungmin repeated, and his smile grew just a little. "You just need chaos and a plan."

chapter thirteen

IT SEEMED, DESPITE THE REPORTED absence of gods on the asteroid, that some higher power had been looking out for the battered party. On the other side of the sealed off doorway, the four women who had beaten them soundly were now fighting a new battle. Aster's scientifically bulky form was struggling now to fix one of the connection boosters that she had set up in one corner of the room. Her large fingers clumsily slapped against each other in her attempt to type on the projected screen. Behind her, Clementine had grabbed Nuwa by the cheek, tugging on the girl's skin mercilessly.

"Where the hell were you durin' that fight?" The bat-wielding woman huffed, piercing eyes filled with annoyance.

"I t-t-thought that you all had it under c-control... Um, we won, didn't we? I thought if I used my power then Miss Louisa might not look so good on the camera. I don't really know anything about filming, but I'm probably just a background character so—"

"Leave her alone, Clementine. The important thing is that she came back to us." Louisa's commanding voice caused her to let go of Nuwa's cheek.

The pink girl fell back onto a pile of gold, causing a large chunk of the treasure to fall on top of her body unceremoniously. The girl pouted and rubbed her cheek. As her pale blue eyes scanned her companions, she buried herself deeper into the pile of gold as though it could hide her away.

"We shoulda held onto that kid. Isn't keeping a hostage, like, a smart thing to do? Leverage or whatever shit they call it," Clementine groaned.

"And have that CoS interfere further?" Louisa sighed. Her gaze was not on her noisy companion. Rather, she was watching Aster's fumbling attempts at reconnecting with a furrowed brow.

"He's the weakest one, right? All those stories said he wasn't even allowed in their last big fight. Sounds like we could take 'em—"

"We're not fighting a CoS." Louisa's voice was sharp and cold, loud enough that Clementine nearly dropped her bat in surprise.

She turned to face Clementine. Her mint eyes were hard and her fingers dug into the flesh of her arms. In the aftermath of the battle, Louisa had taken the time to redo her hair and makeup, saying that she did not want Lady Masamune nor the others that were watching to see her so *vulnerable.* It was one thing to look weak in front of Lady Masamune, but the importance of that broadcast was not lost on her. Those who were observing weren't simply an audience. They would be the potential investors in Lady Masamune's plans if they proved they could take the compass. The strength and worth of Lady Masamune's goals relied on their ability to get the compass and show that they had the power to do so easily. But the appearance of not one, but two, CoS...

"Lady Masamune would not wish it."

"Just sayin', if we brought her back a CoS, then she'd have a legendary weapon. I'd fucking take that gift in a heartbeat," Clementine grumbled.

"Would you all please be quiet?" Aster's mechanical voice was now gravelly and deep, like an old computer struggling to boot back up after overheating. "I have almost fixed the problem. Louisa, if you would like to take your position back by the chest..."

With an offhand wave, Aster motioned in the general direction of the treasure chest, which had been put back on a newly remade pile of gold and jewels.

"Of course. Clementine." Louisa took a step forward. She looked from the golden rings on her fingers, to the slight glint of wires that had covered the entryway. "These rings are set to maintain that barricade. All you must do is hold them and stay still. Do you think you can handle such a difficult task?" By the end of her words, her voice was dripping with venom, and Clementine shuddered before holding out one hand.

"Aye aye, Captain," Clementine replied with the air of a child who had just been given a chore. As the golden rings fell into the woman's hand, she moved into the background and closer to the barricade. "Sure, make me stay in the background. Why don'tcha just put me in the corner like a fuckin' uncool mom—"

"What was that?" Louisa called sharply, and Clementine tensed.

"Nothin! Go do you!"

Louisa shook her head and resisted the urge to roll her eyes. Instead, she walked back up to the treasure pile. Her purple dress shimmered just as brightly as the gold   that rose to her chest, but her attention was not on the splendor around her. Louisa merely took in the sight of the chest, the plainness of it and the basic lock that had been placed on it. All of their research and Lady Masamune's efforts had led to this moment. Though her heart pounded in her chest, she couldn't help but muse on the surprising lack of obstacles in place. The stairway they had taken down had no monsters or traps. The straightforward signs had led them down the tunnel and to the treasure room. And here, in this room, all the treasures were displayed for the taking. The chest, the center-most item in the room, had a brilliant magical light shining upon it to show that it was the true treasure. It was all so simple that some part of Louisa felt nervousness setting in, but she was quick to brush it off. This was all a gift to her, and a gift to her mistress.

"I'm ready to begin," she said aloud, and gave a practiced smile as she heard the chime of the broadcasting eye starting back up.

THERE was no chance of backing out now. Sungmin watched each member of the group as they prepared for the plan that he had laid out. Something familiar turned in his gut, but it was easily dismissed. He tilted his head in the direction of the treasure room instead. His eyes closed as he focused on hearing, and soon enough, he heard the heartbeat of Clementine. Everyone in the universe had a unique sound, a singular song, tied to them. Whether it beat in time to their heart or was a symphony of all that they were made up of, Sungmin would hear it. And right now, he could hear the sound of the rings in

Clementine's hand grating against each other as the woman absently played with them. He could hear the sound of the wires making faint clinking sounds as the woman's actions slightly changed their positioning every time. She was only helping them. The grey-haired musician opened his eyes and looked back to Aquila. He gave the green-eyed trickster a nod. An excited grin spread across Aquila's features. They gave a nod back, albeit theirs were an abundance of energetic bounces of the head. In an instant, their body had shifted and changed. Their earlier conversation still rang in Sungmin's head.

Aquila, can you turn into anything gooey? Or liquidy?

Well, I can turn into that ooze now—

Something else.

Aw, you're no fun. Well... ooh! I can actually turn into—

Aquila's form had melted away into a watery and vaguely humanoid shape. The newly formed water elemental gave the group two thumbs up, then fell apart and splashed to the ground. The puddle began to move like a snake along the hall floor until it slithered neatly through one of the tiny openings between the wires. As their form disappeared to the other side, Sungmin heard Roanoke suck in his breath beside him. He could hear all of their pounding hearts echoing against his slow one. Unseen, the smallest of smiles spread across his features.

ON the other side of the barrier, Aquila crawled their way over to where Clementine was standing. The bat-wielding woman's face was full of absolute boredom as she watched Louisa launch into her new performance.

"What you saw earlier, Lady Masamune and her followers, was a fluke. But notice how we have taken care of the issue swiftly? That is the power of her attendants. Now... "

Clementine began to yawn, but quickly covered her mouth with her free hand to catch the action. She didn't feel like getting scolded anymore than she had been already. The gold rings in her hand felt a little heavier and Clementine couldn't help but look down at them with a frown. The fact that Louisa had given them to her to hold onto, even for a brief span of time, was confusing to her. Clementine knew how much they meant to the uptight woman...

Behind Clementine, Aquila's form had grown back to that of the humanoid shape. A wide grin, created by a parting of the water, spread unnaturally across the creature's face. In a smooth motion, Aquila's watery form stepped into Clementine and covered her from head to toe in the water, practically sucking her in.

"Glug glug, fother-mucker," the trickster whispered in sinister delight.

Caught in a form-fitting drowning suit, Clementine gave an instinctive gasp of surprise—and instantly found herself fighting for breath as the water caught in her lungs. Panic passed over the woman's sharp features as she began to flail madly. The rings were discarded immediately as water-covered hands attempted to move to yank off the water around her mouth.

The sound of the rings hitting the floor and Clementine's arms hitting the gold piles around her quickly grabbed the attention of the rest of the room. Louisa whipped around and stared with wide-eyed confusion at the scene that was playing out. Aster, still enormous, began to take two lumbering steps towards the woman. Nuwa, safe and protected in her golden cocoon, saw this and merely buried herself further into the treasure sanctuary.

"Clementine, hold on! I shall... I shall figure something out!" Aster's voice reverberated around the room, causing more piles to fall about.

The pile that the chest was on collapsed and the chest began to roll. Still, Aster continued towards her teammate. She reached Clementine and began to wrench at the woman's watery suit in a similar fashion as the other was. She was just as successful as Clementine, and she gave a shout as the water splashed all over her body. The technological veins that still ran throughout her form sputtered at the contact with water. The bulky woman took a few steps back as she noted the danger. As she was pondering her next step, however, a heavy silver chain wrapped several times around her large body. Her arms were sealed tightly against her side, preventing her from any sort of flailing.

"Stay put." Roanoke's cool voice broke the silence.

He stood, holding the long silver spiked chain firmly in his hands. Aster gave a screech of frustration and attempted to take a step towards the man, but a small smirk passed over his features as they did.

Roanoke. Do you want to take out the one who hurt Kaleida?
Yes.
Do you want to use your musical channeling without fear?
Yes.
Do you trust me?
...For now.

Roanoke's rainbow eyes glowed in time to the gemstone on his fetter. Around the room, an energetic and powerful techno-beat began to play. It was a perfectly suitable battle song and, briefly, the four women stopped to take it in. Aster stared at Roanoke, her advanced mind racing to process the new development and what it could mean.

"Are you—?"

Though Roanoke could not hear the music, he could feel the power emerging. From Roanoke's gauntlet, bright rainbow electricity shot out and traveled along the length of the whip. As it reached Aster's dampened form, the sound of wires frying and the scent of skin burning joined the song. Aster's scream was piercing as her body convulsed in uncontrolled movements, though she was still limited due to the hold of the whip. As the electricity came to an end, Roanoke flicked the weapon and sent Aster rolling into a pile of treasure.

As Louisa witnessed two of her team members struggling, the woman swore under her breath and raced for her rings. Just as her fingers were about to touch them, a sudden gust of wind sent them flying off. They rolled until they landed at the bare feet of the fabulous peacock. Louisa slowly raised her head to look up at his obnoxiously haughty smirk.

"Hello, peasant," Mayura said in a manner that suggested he had practiced his entrance lines beforehand.

"You—" Louisa's words were cut off as she noticed the torn up papers left on the ground from the earlier fight glow with prismatic power.

I want to help, but I've only got a few papers left, Sungmin. That's like, a few bullets.

Can you use the ones still in there?

Sure, but they won't be super useful as messed up as they got.

What about some paper cuts?

...Oh yeah. I can do that.

Kaleida stood behind Louisa, a wide grin on her features. With one hand outstretched and one hand on her hat, she certainly looked like a true adventurer. "I told you we'd be taking that chest."

The papers rose in the air around Louisa, who stared for only a moment before attempting to plunge after her wires. At the same time, the paper shards dove at her. Red-tinted paper flew through the air as small cuts began to cover the woman's form. Louisa gritted her teeth through it, refusing to acknowledge the pain. Her hands felt around the floor, trying to grasp at the rings she knew were there even as the paper swarm covered her vision.

It was then that Aquila finally fell back off Clementine. Shifting back into their regular form, they sat on the floor and wiped a bit of moisture off their brow. A crooked grin decorated their tanned features.

"Wooo! " they mused to themself, only to find Clementine staring down at them with her spiked bat raised in the air.

"You bitch...!" Clementine sputtered through ragged breaths, still utterly soaked.

A sharp and shrill whistle caught the woman's attention. With a slow and deliberate turn of her head, she reluctantly pulled her gaze off of Aquila to see what asshole would dare whistle at her. Standing several feet away was the team wyvernboy. A dorky grin adorned his features and his pose was similar to that of Kaleida's as his five remaining cards hovered in the air in front of him.

I'm in the same boat as Kal. I got five cards left.

That's perfect, isn't it? You can see the five at once and pick the one you need.

But if I pick the wrong card then I'm gonna be useless—

You have more than luck on your side, Myth. You have us. Please, tell me about these cards.

Myth exhaled as his golden-brown eyes took in each of the cards. Three hearts, one spade, one club. He would have normally picked the spade. The seven of spades would have created seven large spears that would have plummeted down into the battlefield. To Myth, the major damage would have been worth it, but Sungmin had said to go for the weaker club card. *Better to focus a weaker power on one than to use greater power on all.*

Taking in the chaotic battlefield around him, Myth was starting to see the man's point. Biting his lip and steeling himself, Myth grabbed the five of clubs as the rest of the cards returned to his hand.

"You got the wrong hand... I mean, I've got the ace, ah... Ya know. I'm lucky," Myth mumbled, realizing he had completely lost the cool line that he had wanted to say. Giving an easy-going shrug, he threw the card in the air. Five club-wielding golems appeared from the symbols on the card. They surrounded Clementine, and the woman gave a squeak.

"Oh, fuck this!" Her shrill voice pierced the battlefield as the golems descended.

Louisa had managed to retrieve her rings as Clementine found herself overwhelmed. Kaleida could maintain the small pieces of paper more easily than any big paper attack, and the leader found herself unable to get free of the paper storm. Her eyes darted about and she noted that Nuwa was still hidden and watching from the gold pile.

Why the fuck would Lady Masamune insist we take her along!? Louisa thought bitterly, but she quickly scolded herself for questioning. She saw the chest still on the floor and rushed towards it, swatting the paper like mosquitoes as she went. Her hands reached the chest and, with a relieved grin, she grasped at it...only for her hands to go right through it.

"This is my introduction, so I suggest you pay attention." Mayura's bold voice drew her attention back to where he had been standing. There, next to him, a curtain of golden feathers parted to reveal Sungmin standing with the chest safely in his arms.

Mayura. The king of illusions.

Ah, someone who knows how to address me.

I'm sure it wouldn't be hard for a king to maintain an illusion while using his air power, correct?

Such a thing is insignificant! Of course I can do it.

Good. Then we'll work on a grand reveal.

Mayura took one step forward, staring directly at the broadcasting eye. Around him, a badly beaten Clementine and an electrocuted Aster could only look on with pained and defeated expressions. From her safety, Nuwa's pale blue eyes followed him with an innocent kind of curiosity.

"My name is Mayura, the Phantasmal Peacock, King of the Air and Illusions, and I am NOT the weakest CoS!"

"And I'm Aquila, the Dynamic Roc, and I'm just happy to be here!" Aquila said, jutting their head into frame.

"Louisa, we gotta get out of here..." Using her bat to prop herself up, Clementine spat out a bit of blood before propelling herself next to Louisa.

"This is far too much for our current resources." Aster's voice glitched and warped, burnt flesh on her body revealing a metallic interior. The massive fighter managed to make her way over to the brown-eyed woman, pausing only to grab the broadcaster, until the three were together.

Louisa trembled at the realization she was being forced to accept. Tapping an app on her watch, she pulled a scroll out of her inventory. Her cheeks burned with shame; she knew that the broadcaster was

still on her and that Lady Masamune was witnessing their defeat. She felt a sob choke in her throat even as she kept a proud expression.

"Very well. But this is not over. Don't expect to hold onto the compass for long." she whispered. "I will remember each of your faces. I will not stop until I take back what you stole from me."

With a dramatic flourish, she released the scroll. A teleportation circle surrounded the group and they vanished from sight. In her gold pile, Nuwa gave a worried gasp and hid herself further.

In the silence that followed, the group slowly came together. There was a shared pondering among them all as they processed what had just happened. It was, ironically, in this silence that Roanoke found sounds returning to him as though someone were gently raising the volume back up. Though no one was speaking, he could once more hear his own heartbeat and the shifting of coins. He could hear the quiet footsteps as his team moved to stand around Sungmin. Without a word, Sungmin held the chest up enough for all to see.

"The compass." Roanoke's voice felt dry and his heart pounded in his chest faster than it ever had during the battle. He looked around at everyone, then settled his gaze back on Sungmin. "You should open it." His features blushed slightly at his own words, but the nodding of the rest of the group helped him feel a little better.

"You are my number one servant now, after all." Mayura grinned, tapping his fan against Sungmin's shoulder. "I will grant you that honor."

Quietly surprised, Sungmin looked between all of them. He felt words of protest start to rise in his throat but, just as quickly, they faded away. He simply gave a nod.

"Here, I got this." Kaleida grinned.

Raising one fist in the air, she slammed it into the lock. It shattered and fell apart to the ground, which caused Mayura and

Aquila to jump in surprise. The pair were unused to the young woman's unnatural strength, and the somewhat unnecessary display of it was icing on the chaotic cake.

Sungmin had taken a step back when the punch landed but managed to hold himself firm. With the lock broken, there was nothing else to do but to open the chest. He brought one gloved hand to the top of it and slowly lifted the lid so that all could see. Everyone's eyes, a sea of vibrant colors, eagerly bore down on the interior of the chest. They all saw, and all felt the sudden plunging of their guts as the realization hit.

"We made a mistake."

chapter fourteen

IT HAD TAKEN THE GROUP ONLY A minimal amount of searching to find the staircase that Lady Masamune's forces had used. Not particularly hidden, there had been a door in the very back with a sign on it featuring a little-used language. A quick scan from Roanoke's Chroniker had translated the words to "EMPLOYEES ONLY." The trek back had been done in desolate silence and all of them seemed to have forgotten that they had missed one pink-haired blue-eyed girl who had remained curled up and hidden within the gold piles.

The group found themselves sitting back at the decrepit diner that had once failed to serve Roanoke, Kaleida, and Myth. In the biggest booth in the space, which was still relatively small by any higher standard, Roanoke and Sungmin sat on one side of the table while Mayura had sprawled out on the other. The peacock man's long legs had taken up all the space immediately upon getting to the booth, and though Roanoke wasn't comfortable sitting close to Sungmin, he certainly wasn't about to accept the peacock man's offer to sit on his lap. A tense silence lingered in the air even as Sungmin had pulled out his tablet.

"Pointless," Roanoke finally groaned, putting his head in one hand. He could feel a headache coming on.

"Absolutely pointless," Mayura agreed, giving a more dramatic groan as he fanned himself.

"So it seems Sinner's Point created that dungeon a long time ago as a place new adventurers could go to test their skill. It failed so badly it was abandoned soon after. One of those cheesy little rest stop attractions that never lasts," Sungmin mused in a quiet tone. He tapped a button on the tablet and the screen projected into the air so that his two companions could see. He had accessed one of those sketchy and ad-covered travel sites and typed in the rest stop's location. "There's the *Wishing you Good Knights* room, the cafeteria with the *Jello-tinous Cubes,* the boss room with the *Terrifying Red Dragon,* and the treasure room filled with—"

"Plastic coins and jewels. Your friend looked like he was going to cry when he realized." Mayura gave a snort, snapping his fan shut.

"And a treasure chest containing a prize voucher." Sungmin shrugged, leaning back into the uncomfortable seating.

"He's still trying to cash it in, isn't he? How old even is it?"

IN the adjoining convenience store, the other three team members found that they had a new battle to contend with. Myth leaned against the dusty service counter, hands clasped together and golden-brown eyes staring straight at the utterly bored-looking young androgynous person before him. Behind him, Kaleida had her arms crossed over her chest and was staring absently at the cigarettes lining the back wall. She didn't smoke, but reading the different enhancements among the cigarette boxes was a good distraction to the frustration she was feeling. Cigarettes mixed with fae plants, kirin dung, and crushed manticore nails... all things she was fairly certain weren't actually safe to put into anything.

"I only heard legends about this voucher existing... we had given up on it so long ago," the person muttered with the driest sense of awe. Their fingers tapped absently against a textbook of some kind, and the wrinkled uniform top with graphic pajama bottoms spoke to their utter lack of excitement about anything related to their job.

Myth's lips quivered. "Yeah, well... There's not an expiration date on it. We completed the whole dungeon all nice and neat. Can't you give us something for the trouble?"

The clerk groaned. "That dungeon hasn't been used in a hundred years. We don't even have a prize wall anymore."

Myth gave an exasperated sigh, nearly hitting his head against the counter as he slumped. "Come on, buddy. Cut me a break. Please."

"We'll take unlimited snacks!" Aquila appeared next to Myth, their arms already filled with so many snacks that they were falling out of the little trickster's arms.

"How about lottery tickets?" Kaleida added weakly.

The cashier looked between all three and threw their hands up in surrender.

"There might be a box of junk... er... prizes... from that time in the back." With a reluctant sigh, the worker shuffled their way into the back room.

"Now see, this is how ya bargain." Myth practically beamed, though it was half-hearted.

"By begging?" Aquila laughed, dumping the snacks into a worn-down basket.

"When you're broke enough, yeah." Myth huffed.

"Here."

The heavy thud of a box hitting the counter brought their attention back. The cashier had set down a cardboard box that had obviously seen better days. A yellow sign slapped onto it read *Lost and Found.* "There's some things from when they were first making the dungeon, I think. Things they found tossed in the abyss with people's *wishes.*"

The three dove at the box like ravenous animals, causing the young cashier to stumble back. Various objects tumbled out of the box as they searched. The items within were covered with a layer of dust that outdid that which covered the convenience store shelves and the action of searching caused a cloud around the group.

"Oooh, there's a CD!" Aquila chirped, holding up the circular device and looking through the hole in the center.

"Geeze, that must have been in there forever. Myth, what about this cool fuzzy dice thing for the RV?" Kaleida tugged out a pair of fuzzy pink dice attached by a string and twirled them around one finger. She quickly lost control of the action, and the obnoxiously bright object flew past them and took out a small stack of candy wands near them. She blushed in embarrassment, quickly rushing over to fix her mistake as the clerk flashed her a disapproving look.

Myth shook his head. A grin was starting to return to his features as something close to normalcy began to return. After everything that had happened and all of the disappointment, messing around in a store with his best friend was like an instant shot of cheer. Even

Aquila's presence hadn't bothered him. In fact, there was something almost fun about them hanging around. "You guys have to really dig down. Everyone knows it's at the very bottom that you get lucky and find—"

The wyvernboy stopped; his mouth dropped. The pair on his sides leaned in and all of them found their features illuminated by a soft prismatic glow.

"Is that—?"

THE awkward silence had returned to the booth. In the absence of conversation, Mayura had decided to find amusement in one of the simplest ways known to life: annoying the Tartarus out of another person. He pulled the napkins out of their holder on the table. Using his wind magic, he sent the napkins expertly onto Roanoke's head. The rainbow-eyed young man had been doing his best to ignore the childish behavior of the other, but his head had gathered a relatively high hat of the brownish paper. His patience hit zero as one of the napkins smacked into his face, and he slammed one hand down on the table.

"Are you trying to start a fight?"

"I'm giving you a hat. I think it makes you look... mature," Mayura purred, a handsome smirk widening on his features. One could practically see the steam rising off of Roanoke's head.

"Play nice, you two. If you're going to act like this all the time, how are you going to travel together?" Sungmin murmured. He had been reading on his tablet once more. Though he had his headphones back on his ears, it seemed that he still had no problem hearing the pair.

Roanoke's eyes widened at the statement and his head snapped back to look at Sungmin with absolute horror. "What? I'm not going to do any traveling with that cocky—"

Mayura, too, looked offended at the idea, though it was Roanoke's words that grabbed his focus. "Cocky? What about you and that sour look you always have!? Your face could shrivel a flower!"

"What does that even MEAN!?"

"You both want to use the compass to get the same person. And besides..." Sungmin sighed, tapping the tablet screen to once more project it into the air. On the tablet screen, a broadcast displaying their battle against the women played on an inter-sphere news site. The headline read: ***WEAKEST COS AND THEIR FOLLOWERS CLASH AT SINNER'S POINT.***

"Weakest?" Mayura sputtered.

"Followers!?" Roanoke sputtered, his voice harmonizing with Mayura's as they shouted at the same time.

"Wow, both wildly off point," Sungmin tapped one part of the news bulletin and read aloud, "With this video evidence, LI Alliances and the P-300 have stated that these offenders have been added to their most wanted lists."

Roanoke grabbed the tablet and pulled it close to his face, glaring at the words as though he could make them go away with his cutting gaze alone. "No! I'm not anyone's follower!" he cried out, voice quivering.

"You'll have a hard time convincing anyone of that now."

Letting the tablet fall back onto the table, Roanoke collapsed back into the seat. He stared straight ahead, past Mayura and the scene around them. His gaze was lost in memory and imagination. The pounding in his heart resounded loudly in his ears and he could feel his breathing grow sharp and uneven. He tried to calm himself down, but it was a difficult effort to accomplish as his thoughts ran rampant. There were too many thoughts and fears to sort out, and his fingers dug sharply into his side as the dizziness set in.

I made a mistake, I made a mistake, I made a mistake...

As the panic attack set in, Sungmin and Mayura were quick to stand up. Mayura seemed to be at a total loss, turning his attention to Sungmin for a sign of what to do. The grey-haired man bit his lip. He was about to speak when he heard footsteps rushing forward.

"Roan?" In a moment, Kal was kneeling in front of her brother. She scanned his features quickly, then looked back at Myth. "Get Lil' Guy. Now," she said.

Without a word, Myth rushed out of the dining room.

"Kal..." Roan wheezed, tears stinging at the corners of his eyes. He opened and closed his mouth several times, but the only sounds that came out were choked sobs.

Kal gently took Roanoke's hands and gave them a squeeze. "I'm here." Her voice lost the previous sharpness and filled with caring warmth. Without looking behind her, she spoke to the others. "Can you guys go wait by our ship? He needs space."

Sungmin nodded and led the two CoS out of the room. Roanoke and Kaleida were left alone in the dining room, and Kaleida continued to maintain her brother's gaze. Her hands kept his nails from digging into his flesh, letting them clutch at hers as much as needed. She had been through this with her brother many times before. At first, the attacks had terrified her. But she knew, beyond everything, that however scared she might be was only a fraction of what her brother felt in the moment.

"Concentrate on your breathing, Roan. Stay with me. Stay in the moment."

Roanoke attempted to follow her instructions and sucked in his breath. As he tried to focus his overwhelmed mind on his breathing, he found that his thoughts slowed little by little. The feeling of Kaleida's hands on his became more apparent. The pattern of his breathing drew him in.

Myth returned, accompanied by the little will-o-wysp. As soon as the orb saw Roanoke, it flew over to the man. Kaleida let go of her brother's hands as the orb settled in them instead. The feeling of gentle warmth and the soothing aura allowed Roanoke to ease further. He held the orb close to his chest and, after a few minutes, had calmed down enough to look at his closest companions.

"We're criminals, Kal. The P-300 says we're criminals," he whimpered, his voice cracking a bit.

A heavy silence fell over them. Kaleida stared at her brother, then looked to Myth. The wyvernboy's features had furrowed as the man was trying to understand the statement. Finding no solution from him, she turned back to her brother and offered him a weak smile. She outstretched one hand and revealed a beautiful compass. Made in silver and inlaid with a Prismatic Core, it shimmered with more energy than either had ever felt before. The needle of the compass pointed out in the direction of their ship.

"We found the compass?" Kaleida offered.

AT the hazard, Sungmin leaned against the creaky ship alongside Mayura and Aquila. His pale red eyes were staring up at the glittering night sky surrounding them. At his side, one hand idly stroked a pocket in his jacket. He felt the outline of a small bottle there, thoughts drifting beyond their present circumstance.

"Is... is he gonna be okay?" Aquila muttered. They had taken a sitting position on the hood of the ship, their bright green eyes still staring at the restaurant. In their arms, a basket of treats was still held tightly.

"Mhm." Sungmin pulled a small bottle out of his jacket. He didn't even look as he opened it and pulled out two pills, which he popped into his mouth. Mayura watched him, expression thoughtful and a little bit dark.

"What are we gonna do?" they sighed. "We didn't mean to make you guys criminals. We didn't mean for anything to happen."

"You said that the wyvernboy found the compass, right? We can't exactly leave without it," Mayura grumbled.

"And we're not giving it up." Kaleida gave them a hard grin as she and the rest of the Hazard trio approached. Roanoke still held Lil' Guy close to his chest and his expression was tired.

"I like to think that pretty much lays out the situation nicely. We should continue any further conversation inside." Sungmin took his headphones off his head and finally looked back at the rest of the group. "The universe knows we're here now. It won't take long at all for the ships to start arriving. And you two—" Sungmin tilted his head to the two CoS, "don't seem to have a mode of transportation."

"And we do." Myth perked up, slapping the hood of the Hazard in triumph. As he did, a burst of smoke escaped from under the hood. With a yelp of surprise, Aquila bolted off of it and behind Mayura. "She's all ready to-"

His words cut off as his soft gold eyes fell upon the new addition to the Hazard. Sitting on top of the roof, dug deep into the metal, was the meteorite sign smiling down at them. Its arrow pointed up to the stars, as though insisting they take off. The wyvernboy, however, gaped at the thing in disbelief.

"I thought you had a ride, not a liability." Mayura's purple eyes scanned the ship with doubt.

"T-That thing! On top o' her! How did–?"

"There's no time for this," Roanoke said wearily, leaning slightly against Kaleida.

"I could try turning into something..." Aquila offered, but Kaleida shook her head.

"As cool as that sounds, I don't think we could all fit on you. Or survive out in the Stardust Sea."

"And I will die before I leave my baby to the sharks." Myth huffed in quiet indignation. He bent over his ship and pet her hood tenderly, "Come on... I'm not giving up on us. We'll get ya out o' here and get that awful thing o' ya," he cooed. Mayura made a face at the scene, but politely hid it behind one of his fans.

Sungmin came up to stand beside Myth. As the man opened the hood back up, he saw the fizzling core in the center. An idea sprouted in the young musician's mind and he turned to face Kaleida.

"It seems like the core is dying. The compass."

Kaleida stiffened, frowning at the man. "What do you want with–?"

"Questions are great when you have the time to answer them." Sungmin held out one hand.

The twins exchanged a look at that. A moment of indecision wrestled between the two before Roanoke finally gave a nod of his head. Kaleida bit her lip, but pulled out the compass and handed it to Sungmin.

As soon as it was placed in Sungmin's hand, he took the Hazard's core out, shoving the compass inside. There was a sudden burst of power at the action, which pulsed past the group. The rather dismal ship seemed marginally more impressive as it glowed with prismatic energy. The engine roared to life and Myth beamed.

"My baby!"

As the man hugged his ship, Mayura rolled his eyes, then saw the flashing of distant lights in the horizon. With gritted teeth, he grabbed the wyvernboy and Aquila.

"Yes, let's spare the happy reunion. Can we get in now?" he snapped, tugging them into the Hazard. Behind them, Kaleida helped Roanoke into the ship.

Sungmin stood alone outside the ship. He stared up at the sparkling sky with his usual neutral expression, but an element of hesitation flickered in his dull eyes.

"This isn't an adventure," he whispered weakly to himself.

"Sungmin! You too!" Mayura's voice rang out sharply, interrupting the quiet contemplation.

Before Sungmin could protest, Mayura grabbed the back of his jacket and pulled him into the Hazard. "My personal servant is NOT going to leave this party!"

THE door to the ship slammed shut. As it sped off into the Stardust Sea, the first of the ships began to arrive at the rest stop. Among the various models, a single colorful ship designed to look vaguely like a dragon landed. From the ship, a tall and toned woman with two long white and green braids stepped out. She rested one hand on a long sword that was hung on her back, taking several steps out onto the pitiful asteroid before stopping and looking around. As she realized that her target was no longer there, an annoyed smile spread across her features. Calmly, she dug in her side pouch for a core that was no longer needed. Letting it drop back in her pocket, she opened an app on her Chroniker and sent a simple message to a contact listed as ***Dumbass Troublemaking Cutie***.

Kaleida. What the fuck.

FUEL
UP ↑

Character References,
The World,
and Thanks

NAME	Roanoke Mochizuki
AGE	84 (early 20's human years)
RACE	Teien
HEIGHT	5'5"
HOME STAR	Tartarus
GENDER	Male

LIKE	Reading/learning, crafting, music, sweet things, cute things
DISLIKE	Sleeping, cocky people, being dirty, loud noises, being touched
ABILITY	Able to instantly craft weapons and items, enchanting them through his fetter, Tokumei. Slightly stronger than the average human

SUMMARY

Roanoke is the practical and quiet brains of the crew. He is haunted by a difficult past that has filled his sleep with nightmares. Raised by his older sister alongside her children on the former prison star of Tartarus, he has always been surrounded by chaotic people which has made him more reserved and patient. Due to his past, he hates being touched unless he initiates it and has issues with feeling dumb if he doesn't know something. He is also socially anxious and has trouble interacting with new people. Despite all of this, however, he has a playful side and a dry sense of humor. He cares for those around him and is extremely protective. His exasperation with his sister and Myth often is compounded by the fact that he gives in to their crazy ideas more often than not.

NAME	Kaleida Mochizuki
AGE	84 (early 20's human years)
RACE	Teien
HEIGHT	5'6"
HOME STAR	Aries
GENDER	Female

LIKE	Adventuring, video games, spicy things, old tales
DISLIKE	Overthinking, inaction, insects, directions, being alone
ABILITY	Able to manipulate paper for a variety of purposes, skilled shotgun-user, a lot stronger than the average human

SUMMARY

Kaleida Mochizuki is the unwavering bundle of chaotic good energy that travels alongside her brother Roanoke. Raised at the P-300 base at Aries by Shikaaree Waxjaba, her life has been filled with first-hand accounts of journeys and heroes. She is passionate, strong-willed, extroverted, and rash. Despite being raised separately from her brother, the two have maintained a close friendship. It is because of him that she has learned to slow down a bit, but she still has a tendency to want to take charge of a situation and barrel forward.
Her best friend is Myth Lawson, who she met while training at a P-300 academy.
Having traveled alongside the two for the past six months on a nearly impossible mission, Kaleida is impatient to get a start on her first real adventure.

NAME	Myth Justice Lawson
AGE	29 human years
RACE	Quarter-elf
HEIGHT	5'9"
HOME STAR	Crazetusk
GENDER	Male

LIKE	Gambling, graffiti art, his ship, pop music (particularly the idol KUMO)
DISLIKE	Being broke, judgemental people, bitter things, working out
ABILITY	Able to manipulate luck stardust, using stardust-enhanced cards to produce a variety of unpredictable effects. In a pinch, his spray paint cans count as a weapon for him.

SUMMARY

Myth Lawson is the easy-going captain of the broken-down Hazard. A happy medium between the twins, he is seen as a sort of big brother to them. Raised at his family's wyvern ranch in Crazetusk along with his many siblings, Myth quickly fell in love with the idea of becoming a star-wandering hero. After one swung by his star, he decided to leave and train at a nearby P-300 academy. He always considered it to be his luck that got him into it, and trained in using it to his advantage while there. Though he is sometimes too submerged in his concept and refuses to acknowledge how bad his ship is, Myth is reliable and down-to-earth. He often frets about money given that Kaleida is bad at budgeting, and he has little income except for what they get as loot from monsters they defeat.

NAME	Sungmin Park (?)
AGE	65 (early 20's human years)
RACE	???
HEIGHT	5'10"
HOME STAR	???
GENDER	Male

LIKE	Sleeping, music, ???
DISLIKE	Being awake
ABILITY	The ability to manipulate others through their internal songs using Resonance, super-hearing, ???

SUMMARY

As you can tell from all of the question marks, Sungmin is a bit of an enigma to the group. After being inadvertently swept up in the group's disastrous twist of fate, he is forcibly inducted into their group. Quiet, logical, and lazy, Sungmin seems unemotional about the world around him. He often sleeps at inopportune times and avoids fighting if he can help it. His ability gives him a more intimate connection to Roanoke, but his true feelings about this are unknown. He goes with the tide, and has unfortunately been swept out to the Stardust Sea.

NAME	Mayura, The Phantasmal Peacock
AGE	??? (appears in mid-20's human years)
RACE	Children of Stardust
HEIGHT	6'2"
HOME STAR	???
GENDER	Gender-fluid (uses male pronouns)

LIKE	Jewels and adornments, birds, performance, luxury
DISLIKE	Dirt, being looked down on, stuffy people, waiting
ABILITY	Can use air and illusion stardust without tiring. Can use some healing stardust. Able to turn into a war fan, and is an adept martial artist.

SUMMARY

The proud peacock of the party, Mayura is initially introduced to the group as Maymay. He is haughty, dramatic, and instantly clashes with Roanoke. Despite seeming selfish and egotistical, he is protective and takes his job as a healer seriously. As a Child of Stardust, Mayura has an infamous past. After being unsealed two years prior to the start of the book, he wandered about causing chaos at various stars before meeting with Aquila. The pair were traveling to find the Wayfinder's Compass to spite the CoS Kani when they were forced to save the group. Though he reluctantly joins the others, he seems to enjoy the attention and fancies them to be his servants.

NAME	Aquila
AGE	??? (appears in mid-20's human years)
RACE	Children of Stardust
HEIGHT	5'3"
HOME STAR	???
GENDER	Nonbinary ((uses they/them pronouns)

LIKE	Traveling, having fun, eating, interesting people
DISLIKE	Conflict, being reminded of their past, staying still
ABILITY	Able to shapeshift into any creature or item that they have personally seen, though any skills or abilities of the base may not transfer to Aquila's shapeshifted form.

SUMMARY

Summary: Aquila is the optimistic and cheerful traveling partner of Mayura. They initially introduce themselves as Aki, though their poor lying skills causes most of the group to assume the name is fake. They get along easily with people, which helps to balance out the peacock's difficult personality. Aquila is far less known than other CoS, leaving much of their past unknown. They seem, however, to be a gentle and kind soul. They dislike conflict and usually let Mayura guide their next steps, happy just to be along for the ride.

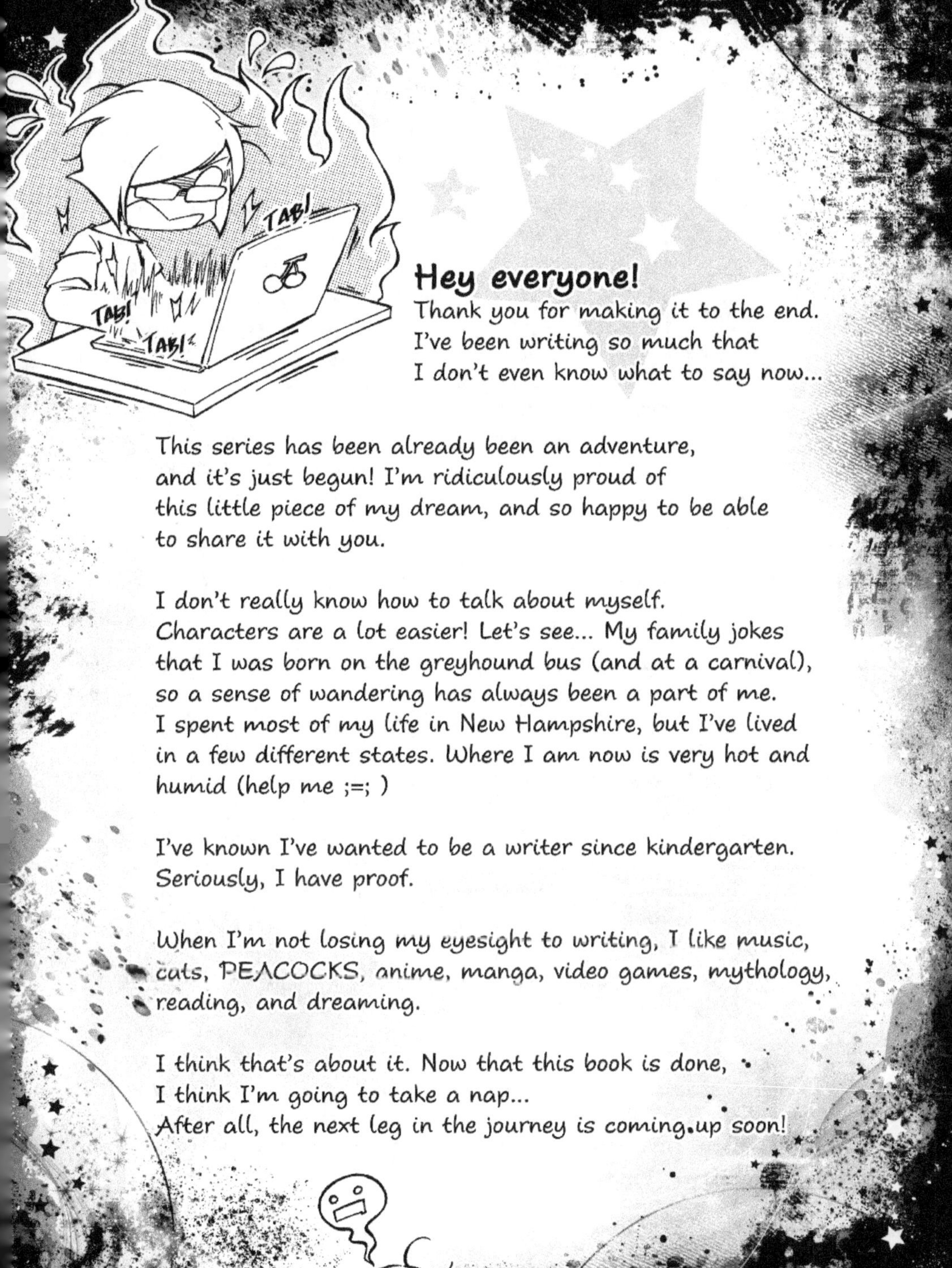

Hey everyone!

Thank you for making it to the end.
I've been writing so much that
I don't even know what to say now...

This series has been already been an adventure,
and it's just begun! I'm ridiculously proud of
this little piece of my dream, and so happy to be able
to share it with you.

I don't really know how to talk about myself.
Characters are a lot easier! Let's see... My family jokes
that I was born on the greyhound bus (and at a carnival),
so a sense of wandering has always been a part of me.
I spent most of my life in New Hampshire, but I've lived
in a few different states. Where I am now is very hot and
humid (help me ;=;)

I've known I've wanted to be a writer since kindergarten.
Seriously, I have proof.

When I'm not losing my eyesight to writing, I like music,
cats, PEACOCKS, anime, manga, video games, mythology,
reading, and dreaming.

I think that's about it. Now that this book is done,
I think I'm going to take a nap...
After all, the next leg in the journey is coming.up soon!

Hello everyone! Um...
You haven't met me yet, but you will
next episode!
I'm here to help out a little bit so
my creator can get some sleep.

My name's Senri, and I travel
the Stardust Sea with my teacher
researching the stars. I bet there was
a lot thrown at you in this book,
so before we get to the glossary on
the next page, I wanted to give you
a little overview.

Children of Stardust is a book series in the universe of Luminary Odyssey.
I guess you could say it's the main one...? (It makes me a little nervous
to know that there may be other troublemakers popping up in other
parts of the Sea...)

The world (re: universe) will hopefully get easier to understand as you read,
but here's the big notes:

The Stardust Sea is what we call everything between the stars. It's like...
Space? But if Space was a lot of drifting energy, like a Sea of energy drinks.
(Now you know why stardust boosters are a thing!). Outside of the Sea is
an area called the Hollow Ocean. It's basically the energy drink can once
there's no drink left. Cold, empty, and a little disappointing.

Stars in the Sea can be the size of a city or the size of continents!
There's also different levels of technology, Stardust, and universal interaction
between them. The best way we've found to organize these stars is to group
clusters of them into things called Spheres.

Just about every star has gods, too. I've been told that can be weird...?
Oh well, I guess it'll make sense the more you read!

And of course, we've got the Children of Stardust. It's sort of a funny name,
if you ask me, because in this universe everyone's basically a child of
stardust in some way. But these beings... These people... They've got a lot
more inside of them than others. And they've got a whole lot more of a history,
too.

Anyways, the glossary coming up should have some
better information.
Thank you, from me and from my creator,
for reading this far!

I can't wait to meet you all officially in the next
episode! (and I'm sorry ahead of time for my teacher)

Children of Stardust: The name given to a mysterious race of beings in the universe. Weapons who can take a human form, they were made by the infamous traitor god, the Wanderer, and were thought to have brought chaos and destruction upon the stars hundreds of years prior. Apparently made from the essence of gods, they were sealed and hidden away until two years prior to the story's start.

Stardust: The latent energy, or magic, that exists throughout the universe. It is in every living and non-living thing, and can be used for various purposes. It is considered to be the basis of existence and is pure until shaped by outside forces.

The Stardust Sea: The name given to everywhere that is between the various stars. It is referred to as a Sea due to being explored using "ships", and the almost liquid-like texture of it that some who have spent time in it and lived reported feeling. Like many seas, one cannot survive being out in it for long, as the high concentration of Stardust can cause bodies to over-stimulate and combust.

Stars: Places that grew around high concentrations of Stardust. They can vary in size from being as small as an island to as large as a continent. Stardust manifests differently for each one.

Gods: Beings on stars that have been chosen, either by the star itself or by other meticulous methods, to be vessels for strong aspects of the star's Stardust variations. Extremely powerful on their stars, their strength plummets when they travel away from their home—which only encourages them to stay on the stars that have blessed them and act as guardians for them.

Teiens: A humanoid race that is on the verge of extinction and flung throughout the Stardust Sea. Much of their history and culture have been lost to time, but it is widely accepted that they have long lifespans, have heightened strength, and are naturally gifted in the arts. They were considered to be master crafters with high levels of Stardust. At one point in time, their god, known as the Wanderer, destroyed their star--scattering them throughout the Sea. With low rates of reproduction and lack of society, the Teiens are rare.

The Wayfinder's Compass: An ancient Teien artifact with the power to find a Child of Stardust and guide the user to them.

The Wanderer: The mysterious god, also known as the Traitor God, whose actions caused the destruction of the star he swore to protect, as well as cause the decline of his race. While there is very little known about him, his creations are both hated and highly sought after. He was apparently defeated and imprisoned somewhere a long time ago, but there are no actual records to confirm this. Still, with no activity for hundreds of years, many assume that he died in one of his last battles against other gods.

credits

Visual Concept Assistance for Roanoke, Kaleida, Mayura, and Aquila provided by Hantueruu on Deviantart

Visual Concept Assistance for Kani, Louisa Concept Design, and Nuwa Outfit Design provided by MagicalEGirl on Twitter

Visual Concept Assistance for Myth provided by Johan Faulstich of Fiendish Fiction

Sungmin Concept Design provided by Chiikun on Facebook

Original Nuwa Visual Concept Design and Postcard Design by Serabourg

Sticker Designs provided by viscereaux (https://viscereaux.carrd.co/)

Button Designs provided by Dreya Nicole, (@adreya on twitter)

Wayfinder's Compass Visual Concept Assistance and Bookmark Designs provided by Shrimpheby on Deviantart

Cover Design provided by Iku-Aldena (https://ikualdena.carrd.co/)

Interior Art provided by Pandabaka

special thanks

Grammy and Grampy: For literally everything. I love you both so much, and I could not be who I am, or be where I'm at, without your lifelong encouragement and support. For listening to every one of my stories, for buying me an endless number of journals to never put them in, and for all the little moments in my life that have made me so happy!

Grammy Joan: I'm sorry I couldn't publish this before you left us for the stars, but thank you for helping me see the magic in them, and the magic in reading.

The Undone Squad: Lindsey, Gus, Jess, Dylan–This story wouldn't be half of what it was without all of you, and I wouldn't be half the person I am. I could never have asked for a more supportive, fun, and absurd space to grow and be welcomed in. You're all so creative, awesome, and caring. Here's to many more adventures together.

To Johan: My oldest (and definitely coolest) friend. I am so proud to have been able to watch you grow, and all the great things you've done. Thank you for challenging me, for helping me, and for always being there in my life. I'm so lucky to have met you, and to be able to call you my friend. (Also, thanks for the COOL belt!)

Thank you, every artist, supporter, friend, critic,
editor, designer.
This book would literally not be without every single one of you.
Thank you for helping this humble dreamer's dream come true.

And thank you, dear reader, for letting my dream into your life...
Even if it's just for a little bit. Wherever our journeys take us next,
I hope we can all find happiness... and our own luminosity.

www.ingramcontent.com/pod-product-compliance
Lightning Source LLC
Chambersburg PA
CBHW051101050726
47592CB00002B/622